Nati was so distracted by the glittery sensation of having Cade's hand on her arm that she completely missed the approach of the kiss.

She didn't know what to do. It seemed as if she should tell him to back off because, along with even bigger issues, he was a client, and their families had bad blood between them.

She didn't say anything at all and instead stood there looking stunned.

"See you," he said, giving her arm another light squeeze before he let go of it.

"See you," Nati echoed dimly.

Nati watched him go, taking in the sight of that rear view that was almost as good as the front. And all she could think was that he had kissed her.

Enough of a kiss to leave her at odds with herself when a voice in her head shrieked, *No!*

And the rest of her whispered, *More…*

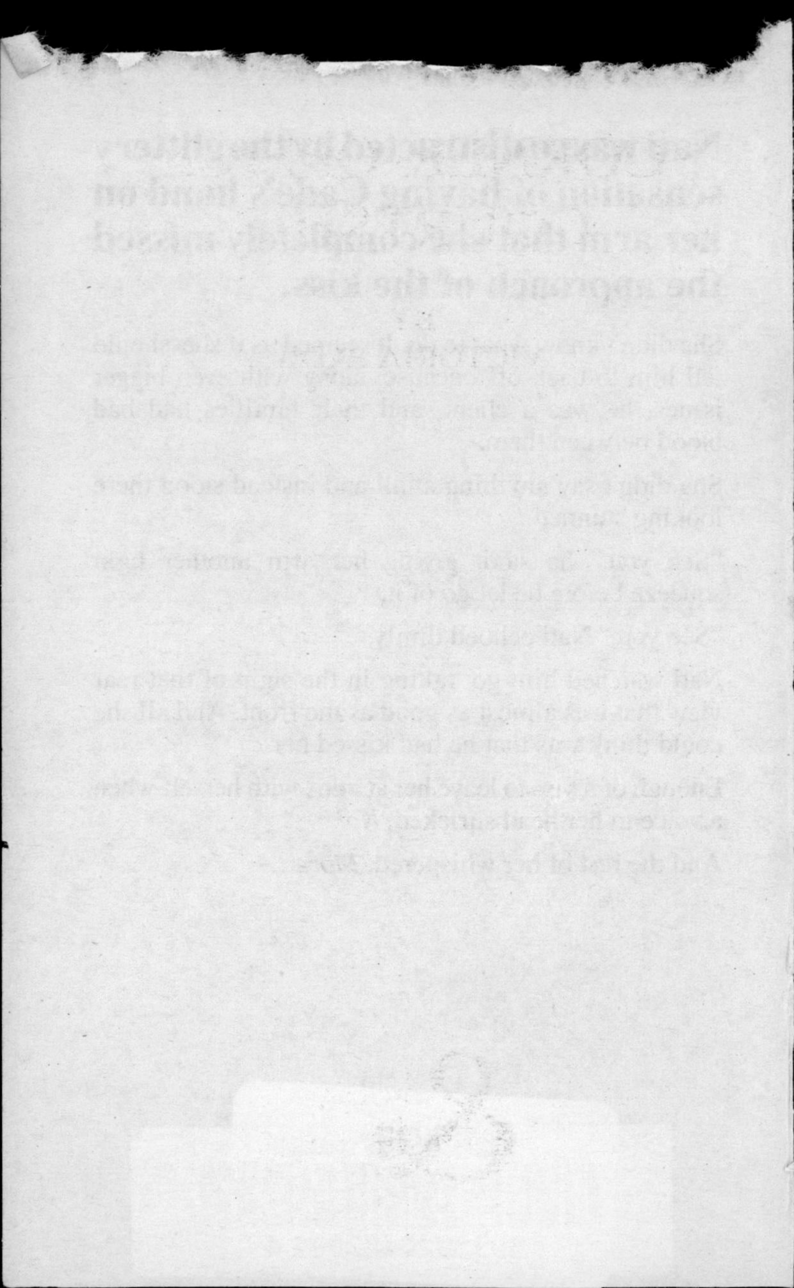

CORNER-OFFICE COURTSHIP

BY

VICTORIA PADE

First published in Great Britain 2013
by Mills & Boon, an imprint of Harlequin (UK) Limited,
Eton House, 18-24 Paradise Road, Richmond, Surrey TW9 1SR

ISBN: 978 0 263 90121 4
ebook ISBN: 978 1 472 00497 0

23-0613

Harlequin (UK) policy is to use papers that are natural, renewable and recyclable products and made from wood grown in sustainable forests. The logging and manufacturing processes conform to the legal environmental regulations of the country of origin.

Printed and bound in Spain
by Blackprint CPI, Barcelona

Victoria Pade is a *USA TODAY* bestselling author of numerous romance novels. She has two beautiful and talented daughters—Cori and Erin—and is a native of Colorado, where she lives and writes. A devoted chocolate lover, she's in search of the perfect chocolate-chip-cookie recipe. For information about her latest and upcoming releases, and to find recipes for some of the decadent desserts her characters enjoy, log on to www.vikkipade.com.

Prologue

"Midnight malteds—there must be trouble," Cade Camden said when he joined his grandmother, his three siblings and his six cousins in the sprawling kitchen of the Denver home where he'd grown up. Georgianna Camden had raised all ten of her grandchildren here after the tragic deaths of their parents.

"Chocolate or vanilla?" she asked without directly responding to his comment.

"Chocolate," Cade answered.

"It's been a long time since one of us got arrested for teenage hijinks," Cade's older brother Seth contributed.

"Nobody died, did they, GiGi?" Lang, one Cade's triplet cousins, asked.

Growing up, whenever there was trouble and the sleepless nights that went with it, they'd all congregated in their grandmother's kitchen. Even if she were angry or disappointed or disgusted with the kids—GiGi had made malteds, done damage control and assured them that they would weather whatever storm came their way.

But tonight, when they'd each been summoned for midnight malteds during GiGi's seventy-fifth birthday party, it set off alarm bells. It was something Cade had been anticipating anyway, ever since GiGi had requested that her grandchildren all spend the night. For old-time's sake…

With everyone gathered around the large island in the center of the kitchen, sipping their malteds, GiGi finally explained why she'd asked them here.

"I've read the journals," she said ominously.

As the descendants of H. J. Camden, founder of Camden Incorporated and the worldwide chain of Camden Super Stores, GiGi's grandkids immediately knew what she was talking about.

Just weeks before Georgianna's birthday, her oldest grandson, Seth, had come across a small trunk hidden beneath the floorboards of the original barn in Northbridge, Montana, where H.J. was born. The trunk contained several journals written in H.J.'s own hand. Seth had immediately sent them to his grandmother.

"This can't be good," Livi, another of the triplets, said softly. Rumors had always flown that Henry James Camden, his son Hank Jr. and even his grandsons Howard and Mitchum had amassed the family fortune by lying, cheating, bribes and much worse.

"It isn't," GiGi confirmed. "I haven't read everything but I've read enough to know that the worst that was ever thought or said about H.J.—and even more—is true."

That sobered everyone in the room.

They all knew that GiGi had never been privy to any of the business dealings, that her response to the rumors and accusations of backroom deals, of misdeeds and wrongdoing had been to instill in her own sons and grandchildren a strong sense of right and wrong. And because H.J. and her late husband Hank had kept business strictly separate from their family life, and been such good and loving heads of the houschold, she'd chosen to believe better of them.

"During those last couple of months after H.J.'s stroke he said some things to me that made me wonder, that made me think he might have reason to feel some shame. But you know he wasn't in his right mind most of that time and so I'd still hoped that the worst wasn't true—"

"But it was," Cade's cousin, Dane, finished for her.

"It was," GiGi said in a dire tone. "H.J. and my Hank especially…." The elderly woman's voice cracked. She shook her head. She clearly didn't want to admit it but she raised her chin and continued, "They trampled over other people to build what we have."

No one said anything to that.

After a moment of collecting herself, GiGi went on. "I'll grant you that much of what was done was done decades ago—your dads put more effort into giving back and sharing our good fortune. But even they…" GiGi shook her head in disappointment. "Well, they still did H.J. and your grandfather's bidding."

"I raised you to be better people and I'm proud of you." GiGi paused a moment, glancing around the island at each of her ten grandchildren and smiling. "But the more I read in these journals, the more I begin to understand the price other people paid for our success and prosperity. We all benefited from what was done. What if the sons and daughters, the grandsons and granddaughters of people taken advantage of by H.J. still suffer? What if these families never bounced back?"

"It's a thought that none of us wants to have GiGi, but—"

"But nothing, Dylan," the older woman said to another of Cade's cousins, using the I-won't-take-any-excuses tone they all knew well. "We need to know just how much damage, how much of a ripple-effect might have been caused. And we need to do something about it."

"You want to make amends?" Cade asked.

"I'll need to do more research, but yes. For my birthday gift, I want each of you to promise me that you'll help find out what the repercussions were for whatever was done so we can atone for the wrongs. Seth, you've already done your part by finding the journals."

"GiGi, we could be opening up a can of worms with this," Cade's cousin, Derek, warned. "If we go around admitting wrongdoing people will come out of the woodwork to make claims—even when there *wasn't* any wrongdoing. We'll have more lawsuits than any amount of lawyers can handle."

"I've thought about that," GiGi said. "It has to be done subtly. With a helping hand here, a good word there. Maybe we'll throw some business in the direction of someone who needs it. Or hire them to come to work for us, or buy whatever they're selling. We'll work behind the scenes—"

"You want us to be manipulative?" Lindie, the third of the triplets, asked.

"Only for the greater good," GiGi answered. "So we can make up for what wrongs were done without opening that can of worms Derek mentioned. And we keep it strictly between us. No one else can know what we're up to."

"I don't know, GiGi," Lang said. "This could be risky. There are people out there who hate us and, now that we know they have real reason to, you want us to stroll in and try to make nice?"

"And without admitting anything wrong was ever done?" Cade added. "As if it's just a coincidence that we're offering something to the family of someone H.J., Gramps, Dad or Uncle Mitchum screwed over?"

"And what if they think we're there to screw them over again?" Dylan contributed.

"It won't be easy," GiGi acknowledged. "And yes, there may be hard feelings and resentments and grudges to deal with. But we're all living the way we do at the expense of other people. Are any of you all right with that?"

In unison, GiGi's ten grandchildren said, "No."

"Of course not."

"You know us better than that..."

"Then we have to make up for it. Carefully. Quietly."

"And you're going to dispatch us each separately, on these...missions?" Lindie asked.

"That's the current plan. And the first *mission*—as you put it—is a matter of the heart. Cade, I'm giving this one to you."

"Great. I get to be the test case."

"Only because you fit the bill, and I'll be paying close attention to putting each of you in just the right situation. Cade, you have that ratty wall in your house with the wallpaper falling off and you need it fixed."

"Oka-ay…" Cade said with reservation.

"There's a small shop in Arden, in Old Town there—"

"It isn't going to look suspicious for me to go out to the suburbs to find someone to paint a wall for me?" Cade asked.

"It's only twenty minutes from here on the highway, and I have it on good authority that the girl who owns the shop does a beautiful job. Her reputation is cause enough to go to her," GiGi said. "Her name is Natalie Morrison. She sells furniture and objects she's painted. It's like folk art. But she also does murals and custom wall treatments. I thought you could hire her to tear off that paper and paint something—"

"I don't want folk art on that wall," Cade said.

"You can have her do something that makes it look like leather or marble or something. And in the process, you can find out what happened after H.J. pulled the rug out from under her grandfather, Jonah Morrison."

"Morrison… As in the Northbridge Morrisons?" Seth asked, connecting the name with the small Montana town where H.J. had begun, and where Seth currently ran Camdem Inc.'s extensive ranching operations.

"Jonah Morrison!" Livi said as if the light had just dawned for her, too. "Wasn't he your first love, GiGi?"

"He was my high school sweetheart," GiGi amended. "Apparently H.J. bought the loan on the Morrison farm and foreclosed on them to make sure that the Morrisons left Northbridge."

"You didn't know that until you read it in the journals?" Cade's younger sister, Jani, asked.

"I was informed that the Morrisons had sold to H.J. I had no idea he'd foreclosed on them. And I thought that the Morrisons left Northbridge by their own choice, that they might be headed to Denver. Jonah and I had already broken up, and I'd met your grandfather by then."

"Then you ended up in Denver, too, and you never looked up your old love?" Lindie asked.

"Of course not," GiGi said. "I loved your grandfather and Jonah was old news. Why would I look him up? But then I read about the Morrisons in the journals and remembered how Maude Sharks recently was bragging at the club about this girl she'd hired to paint the nursery in her daughter's house—"

"This Morrison girl?" Cade asked.

"It was like fate shining a light on what we needed to do first," GiGi marveled. "I did some digging and sure enough, Natalie Morrison has family roots in Montana and a grandfather named Jonah. So that's where we start. Where *you* start, Cade."

"With me hiring your old flame's granddaughter to fix my wall," Cade concluded without enthusiasm.

"And in the process, find out what ever happened to Jonah and if having his family's farm foreclosed on by H.J. was a blessing or a curse. For him and for the family that's come after him—including this girl."

"If it was a curse, what then?" Cade's brother, Beau, asked.

"We'll be giving Natalie work and we'll figure out what else we can do to make things up to her and the rest of the Morrisons," GiGi said confidently. "It'll be up to Cade to figure all that out through the girl."

For a moment no one said anything as the full impact of what they'd learned settled over them.

Then Cade took a deep breath, sighed and said, "So I guess I'm up to bat.... Happy birthday, GiGi."

Chapter One

"Oh, you aren't real, are you—from outside I thought you were…"

Only when Nati Morrison heard the man's voice did she remember how she'd positioned the life-size scarecrow she was working on behind the checkout counter. Nati wasn't visible to the man; she was sitting on the floor behind the counter, sewing straw to the inside hem of the scarecrow's skirt.

She couldn't see her visitor, but it could be Gus Spurgis, the Scarecrow Festival's organizer, bringing her fliers for the October festivities. She decided to joke with him.

In a silly voice, she said, "May I help you?" and pushed forward on the pole running up the scarecrow's back to animate her.

There was no immediate response.

Then Nati looked up, and there, leaning over the

counter, was a complete stranger—not Gus Spurgis. Instead it was a man with a staggeringly handsome face and the most beautiful blue eyes she'd ever seen.

He smiled. "I hope you don't pay your receptionist much—she's a little stiff. And kind of freaky."

"She does work cheap, though." Nati played along as she got to her feet.

And took in the full picture of the man in the business suit standing on the other side of her counter.

Tall, broad-shouldered, with the body of an athlete, he had dark brown hair the color of bittersweet chocolate; a long, slightly hawkish nose; just the right fullness of lips; and a pronounced bone structure that included a finely drawn jawline and chin. It all came together with those incredible cobalt-blue eyes to make him so good-looking that it left Nati a little breathless.

And since he also seemed vaguely familiar on top of it she was lost for a moment in wondering where she might have seen him before.

But she decided she must be imagining things. She was sure that if she had ever—ever—encountered this particular man before, there wouldn't have been anything vague about the memory.

After a moment, she pulled herself together to stop staring at him, and returned to the subject of her scarecrow.

"Freaky, huh?" she mused, glancing at her handiwork. The scarecrow had a real-looking painted clay face surrounded by hair made of straw, a puffy calico dress with more straw sticking out at the wrists and bloomers that came out from beneath the hem of the dress to form legs. “Since I sculpted and painted the face in my own likeness, I think I’m insulted.”

“It’s interesting—I’ll give you that. But you didn’t do yourself justice.”

Was that a compliment or a comment on her sculpting skills? Nati decided not to take it personally one way or the other. “It’s supposed to be sort of a caricature,” she explained. “I know my nose turns up a little at the end—”

“Just enough to be kind of perky,” the man said, his gaze going from her nose to the scarecrow’s.

“But in order to exaggerate it, I gave her a ski-jump nose,” Nati went on. “And I’m grateful that I don’t have that pointy of a chin—”

“No, your chin is just fine… Delicate. Nice…”

She hadn’t been fishing for compliments but she was flattered.

He went on with his critique. “And you definitely missed on the mouth. Yours is good—you have nice, full lips. But that’s one tight-lipped smile on the scarecrow.”

Her chin was delicate? Her lips were nice and full?

Nati felt some heat come into her face even as she told herself that it was silly. There was nothing flirtatious about what he was saying or the way he was saying it. Was there?

It had been a long time since a man other than her grandfather had noticed much of anything about her, and maybe it was going to her head. Just a little.

It was silly, she told herself again. Silly, silly, silly. They were just making small talk.

Her shop door opened just then and a tiny, frail old woman came in.

"Hi, Mrs. Wong," Nati greeted, glad for the distraction. Then she said to her male visitor, "If you'll excuse me for a minute. Feel free to look around..."

Turning her back on the man, who was somehow managing to unnerve her without even trying, Nati grasped a small cheval mirror and brought it around to the front of the counter.

"Oh, that's just beautiful!" Mrs. Wong said.

She had brought the heirloom to Nati to restore the painted ivy decoration on its frame.

"I'm just amazed," the older woman said. "There wasn't much more than a shadow left and you brought it back to life. It's as pretty as it was the day my father gave it to me—that was seventy-two years ago."

"I'm glad you like it. Let me carry it out to the car for you."

"Why don't you let me do that?" the male customer offered.

"No, that's okay, it isn't heavy," Nati assured him.

But she had an ulterior motive. As she carried the mirror out to the elderly woman's car parked at the curb, Nati took a peek at her own reflection, making sure her appearance compared favorably to the scarecrow's.

She'd worn her chin-length, golden-brown hair loose today, just barely turned under at the ends. She would have liked it if she had a comb to run through it to neaten it up a little. As it was, her swept-over bangs were falling a bit in her face.

She had on her usual makeup—a little pinkish powder she'd brushed onto her apple-round cheekbones, a little mascara to bring out her brown eyes, and although she'd applied a light lipstick when she'd left the house this morning, it was four in the afternoon and it was long gone.

She was wearing jeans and a T-shirt that suddenly seemed awfully plain and maybe a size larger than necessary. She was comfortable, but now she would have liked to look more stylish. And maybe show off some of her curves.

But still, as she slid the mirror onto its side into the backseat of Mrs. Wong's car, she decided that she wasn't too much the worse for wear.

She was better off than the scarecrow.

Not that it mattered. The guy was only a customer, she reminded herself. At least she thought he was. Whatever his reasons for visiting her shop, they weren't about her personally.

Once she'd made sure the mirror was secure, she closed the car's rear door and turned back toward her shop, noticing that while Janice Wong was browsing through the painted and stenciled tole pieces she had for sale, the good-looking guy was watching her through the plate-glass windows. Rather raptly…

At least he was until she caught him at it, and then he glanced away.

Maybe he was a summons server and he felt guilty about what he was really there to do….

There *had* been a summons server from the Pirfoys' attorneys at the start of the divorce, who had acted a little like this guy…

But the divorce was final. The settlement had been signed. The almighty Pirfoys couldn't come back and try to take anything else from her or from her grandfather, and surely Doug wouldn't be bothered doing anything else six months after the fact, would he? Especially when the divorce had been so much to his advantage.

No, she was just being paranoid.

First she had been silly to think something was clicking with this perfect stranger—even though she wasn't in the market to *have* things click—and now she was afraid the guy was there to cause her some kind of problem.

She must be delirious. That's what she got for eating nothing but gummy bears for lunch.

"All set," Nati announced to the older woman as she went back into the shop.

"And I paid you in advance, didn't I?" Mrs. Wong asked.

"You did. You're good to go."

"I'll make sure my neighbor is careful when he takes the mirror out of the car and brings it in for me," Janice Wong promised. "And I just might come back another day for one of those old tin coffeepots—they're so cute!"

"I'll be here," Nati assured her, holding the door open for the tiny woman.

Then she turned her attention back to the man…

"I'm sorry for the interruption," she apologized. "But now I'm all yours—" She cut herself off the minute the words came out. But she couldn't help it—she warily enjoyed the sight of this gorgeous guy's amused grin. She liked how the small lines crinkled at the corners of those excruciatingly blue eyes of his.

"What can I do for you?" she finally asked.

"I'm looking for Natalie Morrison."

Summons server.

Nati felt dread run up her spine.

"You found her," she said, going back behind the counter where she felt somehow safer. "It's Nati, though. No one calls me Natalie."

The man did not bring an envelope out of his breast pocket. Instead he merely said, "Okay, Nati. I'm Cade Camden."

Not a summons server—that was good. But a *Camden?*

That was why he looked familiar. They'd never met but pictures of the Camdens showed up in newspapers and magazine articles periodically because they were one of Denver's preeminent families. There were a lot of them, so Nati couldn't have put a name with any of the faces, but she had seen the faces. And she certainly knew the family name.

Her own family's first negative encounter with the wealthy had been with H. J. Camden. He was the reason the Morrisons moved to Denver in 1950, the reason behind Nati's great-grandfather losing his farm and needing to pack up his wife and son—Nati's grandfather—in order to find work beyond the confines of the small Montana town where he was born. It was a story she'd heard numerous times.

But did Cade Camden know it? And what was he doing in her shop? Looking for her specifically?

Nati considered battering him with questions.

She considered throwing him out of her shop in honor of those who had come before her.

But instead, with more reserve than she'd shown so far, she repeated, "What can I do for you, Mr. Camden?"

"Call me Cade."

Nati didn't do him the courtesy of saying his name. She merely waited for his answer, not quite sure how to feel about a Camden standing right there in front of her.

"I bought a house not long ago," he said. "It has a wall in the dining room that has the most hideous wallpaper you've ever seen. It's ripped and peeling and falling off. The wall underneath looks like it could be kind of a mess, too, and I've heard that you can do wonders with wall treatments—not stenciling or anything frilly, but something understated, classy."

"How did you hear about me?" she asked, and this time she *was* fishing.

"I believe you did something in a nursery for one of my grandmother's friends. You come highly recommended."

Nurseries were a large part of her business outside of the shop, so that claim was feasible. But it didn't explain whether or not he knew about their families' past.

Knowing who he was and what he said he wanted was a start. But Nati contemplated a few more things as she studied him.

She considered saying she was too busy and didn't have time for a project like that now. And then recommending someone she knew would botch the job.

She considered taking the job and charging Cade Camden an arm and a leg, effectively cheating him to get even in some small way.

But in the end she didn't like what that approach would say about her own integrity. Having a clear conscience was more important than making some sort of petty point with this stranger who was generations away from the man who wronged her great-grandfather decades ago. A stranger who might not even know what had gone on.

She could merely refuse to work for him, she told herself, and send him on his way.

But her shop had only been open a few months and she wasn't in any position to turn away work. She needed any money she could make. And Camden or not, he was offering her a job.

"I'd have to look at the wall," she said without enthusiasm. "I need to see what kind of shape it's in before I know what will need to be done and how much it might cost. Plus we'd have to talk about your preferences—different textures and finishes take different amounts of time, so labor charges can add up."

"Sure," he said, seeming undaunted by the potential expense. The Camdens were rich enough to buy and sell her a billion times over.

"Is there any chance you could stop by tomorrow?" he asked. "Maybe late in the day, after you close up here and I get home from work?"

"I can come anytime." Nati nodded toward the double pocket doors to her right, just behind her counter. They were open, exposing the shop next door. "I'm friends with the owner of the Pet Boutique. Whenever one of us needs to be away we open those doors to connect the two stores and take care of both shops at once—I'm doing that right now while Holly goes to the bank." Too much information.

"And you're free tomorrow?"

Nati didn't have to check anything to know that she was. "Just tell me what time's good for you."

"Six-thirty? I'm in Cherry Creek, just past the Denver Country Club, off University, if that's okay."

"Sure," she said. "But aren't there people in your neck of the woods—"

"Like I said, you came highly recommended and I want it done right."

"Okay," she said, wondering why she was feeling let down that they'd gone from the easy banter about the scarecrow to this all-business approach.

But all business—*only* business—was how it should have been from the start. And now that she knew who he was it was certainly how it would be from here on.

He gave her his address and directions to his house. Then he said, "Tomorrow night, six-thirty. I appreciate your coming that late, on a Friday night. I've been trying to get in here to meet you all week but I've had too many fires to put out at work and this was my first chance. It shouldn't waste too much of your night to just take a look, though."

If only he knew that she spent most Friday nights—and every other night of the week—painting inventory to sell in her store.

But she wasn't going to tell him that. "It's fine. No problem," she assured.

He should have left then. But he stayed staring at her for another moment before he said, "When my grandmother's friend told her about you she gave her your card. The name rang a bell. My grandmother said she knew some Morrisons a long time ago. Jonah Morrison in particular. When she lived in—"

"Northbridge. In Montana. Jonah Morrison is my grandfather," Nati said pointedly.

"Small world..."

So was this a coincidence?

Somehow that seemed farfetched to Nati.

"Well, then," Cade Camden said with a sigh, "I guess I'll see you tomorrow night."

Why did it seem as if he was looking for an excuse to stick around?

But Nati wasn't going to give him any reason to. Even if there were an infinitesimal part of her that wanted to.

Instead she said, "Six-thirty. I'll be there."

"I'm looking forward to it...." he said almost more to himself than to her.

Then he walked out into the bright October sunshine of a Colorado day while Nati watched him go.

And as she did, she recognized some very conflicting emotions roiling around inside of her—among them what seemed like it might be an eagerness to see Cade Camden again.

But she mentally stomped the feeling out like a cinder from a campfire.

At least she thought she did.

Until a moment later when there it was again...

Chapter Two

"Here's the material for the next… And there you are again—this is the third time I've come into your office today and found you staring into space with that weird little smile on your face."

Cade glanced in the direction of his open office door, where January was standing in the threshold.

His little sister was right: every time she came into his office today, she'd caught him staring into space. He'd basically wasted this entire day. He seemed to have Nati Morrison on the brain.

As for his smile?

He hadn't even been aware of that….

"What are you daydreaming about?" Jani demanded.

"Ah, it's just… You know… Nothing. It's been a long week, it's Friday, I guess my brain is starting the weekend a little early and taking me along with it."

"Do you have big plans?"

"No. In fact I don't have any plans." He glanced at his watch. "Oh, but I do need to get out of here. I have that Morrison woman coming by the house to look at the wall and my place is a mess."

"That Morrison woman…" Jani repeated, coming in and closing the door behind her.

All week long the Camden grandchildren had been discussing what their grandmother had asked of them. But they were always careful to do it so that nothing could be overheard.

They all agreed that amends should be made. But no one was eager for GiGi to send them on their particular missions. So there was some sympathy in Jani's expression when she turned back to Cade as he began to clear his desk to leave.

"So you finally met her?" Jani asked, her voice somewhat hushed, even though there was no need to whisper. She'd crossed the office to stand facing Cade at his desk.

"I met her yesterday," Cade confirmed. "You know what this week has been like—I didn't get over to Arden until late yesterday afternoon."

"How did it go?"

"Okay, I suppose. It was great until I introduced myself. Then things cooled—we were joking around a little but when she found out who I am… Well, like I said, it got a little chillier."

"Did she throw you out of her shop?" Jani asked with some dread, as if she were thinking ahead to what she might encounter when it was her turn to do a good deed.

"No, but she might have thought about it," Cade said. "There were a couple of pauses when I half expected her to unload on me or kick me out or something. But instead she just got less friendly, more businesslike."

"So it was *friendly* before she knew who you were?"

"Yeah. Nati Morrison seems really nice. Sweet. Funny—"

"You liked her…."

"Sure. Yeah. You know…" Cade hedged.

"Pretty, nice body, if you'd met her in a bar you'd have bought her a drink?" Jani probed.

Cade laughed. "Probably," he admitted, not telling his sister that in fact Nati Morrison was beautiful. And cuter than hell when she smiled and a tiny dimple appeared just above the right corner of her mouth.

He also didn't tell his sister that Nati Morrison had silky, shiny hair. Or that she had flawless alabaster skin with a healthy little pink blush to high cheekbones. Or that she had a nose most women he knew would have paid good money to have surgically produced for them. Or that her lips were lush and lovely, and her big, round eyes were the color of the finest topaz—brown and bronze and gold all at once—incredibly beautiful, with long, long lashes.

And the body that went with it wasn't bad, either—she was a compact thing at not much more than five feet three inches, with curves in all the right places and a tight round backside….

"Cade?"

Jani's voice barely got through to him.

This was crazy—he kept zoning out into Nati Morrison Land…

He had no idea what his sister had just said, if she'd said anything at all.

"Sorry. Like I said, I'm in outer space today," he apologized.

"I said that she must have at least some idea about what went on between H.J. and her family."

"She knows that GiGi and her grandfather knew each other in Northbridge—I mentioned it and she finished my sentence. Whether or not she knows anything more than that is still a question. She could just be one of those people who doesn't like us—you know how that is."

They were all well aware of the two camps of opinions about their family—there were those who admired, respected and appreciated what the Camdens had achieved. And there were those who envied and hated them, and contended that their fortune had been built on the backs of the "little people."

"Right," Jani said, "Camdens are either titans of industry or despicable robber barons."

"And sadly now we know that there could be some truth to that second opinion," Cade muttered.

"Yeah," Jani muttered. "But Natalie Morrison *is* going to do your wall?"

"I think so. That's what she's coming over to look at tonight. Then I suppose she'll give me a price."

"A million dollars?" Jani joked.

Cade laughed. "I guess we'll see. That *would* be a way to get even with us."

"Well, you better not keep her waiting," Jani advised. Then she held up the papers she had in her hand. "This is the material for the next board meeting—that's why I came in here in the first place. To find you lost in thought with a smile on your face—I'd forgotten about that smile…." Light seemed to dawn in Jani. "Is *that* what you're thinking about today? And smiling about? Natalie Morrison?"

"Nati. She doesn't like to be called Natalie." He had no idea why he was correcting his sister.

"You've been sitting around here daydreaming—and smiling—about *Nati* Morrison?"

"Nah! I told you, it's just been a long week and my brain has been checking out today."

"Mentally checking out Nati Morrison," Jani goaded.

"Just give me the papers and get out of here so I can go home," Cade countered, snatching the sheets from his sister's hand.

"Home to Nati Morrison," Jani teased like the incorrigible younger sister she could be.

"Home to see what I can do to make up for the sins of our fathers. Don't get cocky, your turn will come."

"I can only hope that my turn turns me on as much as yours seems to be turning you on."

Cade laughed wryly and shook his head. "I'm not turned on by anything about this chore GiGi has me doing."

"If you say so…" Jani teased again as she headed for his office door.

"I say so," he insisted just as she went out, shaking his head again at the idea that anything about the situation with Nati Morrison was turning him on in any way.

Sure she was a pleasure to look at. She'd also been a pleasure to banter with yesterday before she'd learned who he was—and not so bad even afterward. But that was nothing.

As the first of the Camden heirs to be doing this

making-amends thing, he was flying by the seat of his pants, writing the rules as he went along. And the biggest rule so far was to be careful.

Which, coincidentally, had become his biggest rule when it came to women in general these days.

But in terms of Nati Morrison specifically, he had no way of knowing what old issues might be brought back to life merely by a Camden showing up, so he had to be extremely cautious. There was already an ugly history between the Camdens and the Morrisons, and he didn't want anything in the present to make things uglier—that would defeat the whole purpose of this endeavor.

For that reason alone, Nati Morrison was not someone he could ever risk getting personally involved with.

But that wasn't his only reason.

Cade finished clearing his desk for the weekend and left his office, telling his secretary to take off early and have a nice weekend.

He headed home with Nati Morrison still on his mind. He tried to think about her in a way that sobered him rather than made him smile.

Yes, the history between their families was a huge concern, no question about it. But on a more personal level, long before he'd met Nati Morrison yesterday, he'd arrived at a firm sticking point in regard to who he would and wouldn't have a relationship with.

It had to be someone who wasn't in a position to see him as her golden goose. Or her winning lottery ticket. Someone who didn't *need* a golden goose or a winning lottery ticket.

And not because he was a snob—GiGi grew up with modest means and had raised him and all the rest of her grandchildren to be anything *but* snobs. She'd be the first to cut him down to size if she thought he was.

But dating exclusively within his own social circle or the very near ripples around it had just become a safety issue for him. An issue of protection. Of self-preservation.

Any woman he opened the door to had to be a woman who was only interested in him for the person he was, regardless of his last name or the size of his bank account.

So he wasn't taking any chances when it came to Nati Morrison. He would do what GiGi wanted him to do, but that was it. He wasn't getting personally involved. He wasn't putting himself at risk.

He'd made that mistake twice before.

No, he told himself as he drove home, as he pulled into his driveway then into his garage, Nati Morrison might be funny and spunky and kind to old women; she might have great hair, great skin, lush lips, beautiful eyes, even a dimple, but it wasn't enough for him to let down his guard.

So get on with this, get it over with, then get out, he told himself.

And that was exactly what he intended to do.

He just wished that his grandmother would have sent him on a mission that didn't include someone whom he'd now spent an entire night and day thinking about.

And apparently smiling like an idiot over when he did....

Nati was five minutes early on Friday evening when she arrived at the Cherry Creek address that Cade Camden had given her the day before.

About a mile east of the Denver Country Club, the house was in a neighborhood comprised of older, upscale homes. Cade Camden's house was a stately redbrick, two-story Georgian with decorative black shutters on either side of the black door and all of the white-paned windows. While it was hardly modest, it wasn't the mansion she'd thought it might be.

For the sake of privacy, the front yard was bordered by redbrick columns and wrought-iron fencing. Two larger columns bracketed a double-car driveway. Nati drove her aging sedan around the block while she tried to decide whether she should pull into the driveway or park in front of the house on the narrow city street.

Nearing the house for the second time, she decided it might be presumptuous to park in the driveway, so she pulled up to the curb and turned off her engine.

Why am I so nervous about this whole thing? she asked herself as she unbuckled her seat belt and gathered the notebook with samples of her work and the pamphlets and fliers about wall textures and colors.

She'd arrived at any number of houses in the last six months to bid on jobs.

But none of those other bids had involved a Camden, she reminded herself.

Cade Camden.

The man she hadn't been able to stop thinking about since she'd first looked up from behind her counter into those amazing blue eyes.

But if ever there was a guy for her to stop thinking about, it was him.

She'd spent a full year under legal siege from her now ex-husband and his family. Barely six months after the divorce, the very last thing she needed was to get involved with another spoiled rich boy and the family that came with him.

And if that weren't enough—and it most definitely was—this particular rich boy was a *Camden.*

If dealing with the power bought by the Pirfoys' money had been daunting, she couldn't even fathom what kind of hell the Camdens could rain down on her.

And the Pirfoys hadn't come with the reputation the Camdens did. Or with the track record the Camdens already had with the Morrisons.

Ruthless—that was what her grandfather had said about H. J. Camden. Whatever and whoever was in H. J. Camden's way got run over, left as roadkill.

And how far from the tree could the apple have fallen? Nati asked herself.

Probably not far. It was unlikely that the Camden stores, the Camden empire, the Camden fortune had continued to thrive without H. J. Camden at the helm because his descendants were nice guys.

And the fact that Cade Camden had *seemed* like a nice guy yesterday?

Her ex-husband had *seemed* like a nice guy at the start, too.

She could still turn this job down, she reminded herself.

Maybe she should....

But her car was sixteen years old and making a bad noise. Plus, she had trouble getting it to start every morning. She had more bills due this month than she had money to pay them, her grandfather's birthday was next month and with Christmas the month after that, there was no doubt that she needed the money this job would bring in. She just plain couldn't afford to turn it down.

And this was just a job, after all. She would do what he hired her to do, get paid and go on her way. What went on in her head in the process didn't matter. It was just a nuisance that she'd have to deal with until it wore itself out. Which she was certain it would do.

She was going to do this job, collect a nice fat check and get her car fixed and pay her bills. And in a way, the fact that Camden money would be paying those bills was a win for the Morrisons. Not that her great-grandparents would have considered it anywhere near restitution, but it was a teeny, tiny win nonetheless.

Nati pulled on the handle to open her car door but nothing happened.

The door needed to be fixed, too, and she suffered a moment of anger, frustration and longing for the luxury car she'd had to leave behind in the divorce.

"Don't pour salt into the wounds," she beseeched the old beige sedan that she'd used in college until she'd married Doug. She'd left it with her grandfather for the six years of her marriage and was now driving it again.

As if her plea had helped, when she tried the door a second time it opened and she got out.

"Thank you," she said to the car when she closed the door, then she headed up the driveway to Cade Camden's house.

There were two steps up to the small landing at the front door where twin marble planters bearing matching topiaries stood like sentries on either side. Nati rang the bell and instantly heard a muffled "Coming" hollered from inside.

A moment later, Cade Camden himself opened the door.

He was wearing suit pants and a white dress shirt with the sleeves rolled to his elbows and the collar button undone. There were some nearly transparent spots on the front of his shirt where water must have splashed him, and he was drying his hands on a dish towel.

"Right on time!" he crowed in greeting. "If you had been ten minutes earlier you would have caught me with dirty dishes in the sink."

"Your maid didn't do them?"

"My maid?" he parroted with a laugh. "I don't have a maid."

"Sorry," she said. "I just figured—"

"They were my dishes from last night and this morning," he explained. "My grandmother would have shot me if she knew that I hadn't rinsed them and put them in the dishwasher when I'd finished eating, but you know how it is—sometimes you just feel lazy…."

"I won't tell," Nati promised, taking stock of his face again and realizing that no, she hadn't been imagining him to be better looking than he actually was—something she was hoping she might have been doing. He was every bit as head-turningly handsome as she'd been remembering him, and he smelled wonderful, too. He appeared to be freshly shaven and the scent of citrus and clear mountain air was wafting out to her.

And weakening her knees a little…

He also had great hair, she realized in that instant. Thick and clean, he wore it cut short on the sides and back with the top just a bit longer but still neat. Not so neat that it looked as if he'd put much care into it, though. In fact, it was just tousled enough to keep him from appearing too businesslike, to give him a casual air. And somehow it made her want to run her fingers through it....

Nati tightened her grip around her notebook and pamphlets as if that was the only way she was going to be able to keep from doing it.

"Come in," he invited then, moving to one side of the entry so she could step across the threshold.

The entry was large, with a steep set of stairs directly in front of the door, a hallway alongside the stairs that was a straight shot to a kitchen at the other end of it, a formal living room to the left and double doors to the right that were open to a library that looked like something out of a Charles Dickens novel—all dark wood, tufted leather seating and books and books and books.

Cade closed the front door. "The wall that needs work is in the dining room—be prepared," he cautioned as he led Nati down the hallway beside the stairs.

Don't look at his rear end...

Don't look at his rear end...

Don't look at his rear end...

Oh, but it was such a good one...

Because yes, despite her efforts to keep herself from doing it, she did look. And whether his impeccably tailored pants did it justice or his backside did the pants justice, Nati didn't know. She only knew that Cade Camden had a very, very fine derriere....

"Nice house," she said, forcing herself to glance at

the big spotless kitchen that showed no signs of having been a mess earlier.

Cade tossed the dish towel on a kitchen counter. “I’ve been here almost a year but I can’t take credit for anything—the couple who owned the place before me had been remodeling it a room at a time. The dining room was last on the list and just as they were getting to it, they split up.” He took her through the kitchen, through an adorable butler’s pantry and into a formal dining room.

There was a long rectangular table with six chairs on each side and one at either head, a sideboard and a tall hutch—all in mahogany. The back wall immediately drew Nati’s attention. The gold-foil wallpaper printed with black safari animals riveted the eye.

“Oh, dear…” she said with an astonished laugh.

“Yeah, I know. Even if it wasn’t peeling off and ripped in spots, it would still be something, wouldn’t it?”

“Do you mind if I tear that piece off a little more so I can see what shape the wall is in behind it?” Nati asked, pointing to one section that was already coming away.

“Be my guest. It’s all gonna have to come down anyway.”

Nati set her things on the dining room table and got to work.

“The paper comes off pretty easily and the wall doesn’t look as if it’s in bad shape, so that’s all good. I’ll need a day to strip the paper and clean up the wall—whatever glue is left will have to be cleaned off so the surface will be uniform and smooth, and it’ll have to be primed. Then I can go to work on it.”

She glanced at Cade and found that he was staring at her, not the walls. "So it seems like something you can do?"

"It does," she answered. "It will take a few days—this wall is big and there will have to be some overnight drying time between coats. But yes, I can do it."

"Music to my ears," he said as if he'd been worried that she couldn't. "When can you start?"

"I'll have to check with Holly to make sure she'll watch my shop but I think I can probably sneak away tomorrow afternoon and get this paper down and the wall primed—that way it will have Sunday to dry and I can come back on Monday—does that work for you?"

"I have to go into the office tomorrow, but I can give you the code to the front door so you can come and go whenever you need to."

That seemed very trusting of him. But Nati was trustworthy; plus, the Camden's probably wouldn't expect anyone to dare do wrong by them.

"Okay," she agreed. "Then I can be here Monday until about one—I have to watch both shops Monday afternoon—and we'll take it from there?"

"Sounds like a plan," he confirmed.

"So let's talk colors, textures and finishes," Nati suggested.

He pulled out a chair for her, and then took the one next to it at the head of the table for himself. Sitting back in the seat, he brought one ankle to rest atop the opposite knee and held on to his shin with a big, powerful-looking hand. Then he laid his other elbow on the table. Nati had an inordinate awareness of the masculine forearm exposed by his rolled-up shirtsleeve, of the thickness of his wrist. Of all things…

Thoughts—these are only thoughts, she reminded herself. *They don't mean anything. Just go on with what you're supposed to be doing....*

She opened her notebook and set out her pamphlets and color choices, telling him what each texture entailed and how it would look.

"I can leave the pictures and the samples with you if you have someone whose opinion or input you might want—a fiancée or significant other."

The thought that there might be someone else had just occurred to her. She'd been assuming that he was on his own because everything he'd said about this project, about this house, had made it sound as if it were his and his alone. But looking at him—nearly drooling over how gorgeous he was and having the mere sound of his voice send goose bumps up her arms—made her realize suddenly that he probably had any number of women he could pick and choose from, and possibly someone he'd already chosen in the wings.

And, yes, she was curious. Even though it didn't matter to her one way or another if he were involved with anyone.

"It's just me," he said. "No fiancée, no significant other."

Nati wondered if she might have stepped in it. "I'm sorry if that sounded like I was prying. I just thought that it's a big house for one person and—" Then she had another thought and instantly said, "Oh, maybe you're recently *out* of a relationship. Or a marriage. Maybe that's why you bought this place—" She stopped herself when she realized she was really being nosy. "It doesn't matter, I was just saying that if there's someone you want to consult with, you don't have to make a decision today."

He was smiling. Her verbal scrambling was funny to him. "I bought the place because I felt like I was ready to take on a house. I liked this one, and it's ten minutes from my office, from my grandmother, from most of my siblings and cousins. I'll rely on your advice when it comes to what would go best in here—I can tell from what's in your shop that you have good taste, I just don't want—"

"Anything frilly. You want something understated and classy." She was repeating what he'd said the day before.

"Right."

"I can do that," she assured him, and went on to make her recommendations, showing him pamphlets that displayed a variety of textures.

"Yeah, I think I like the Venetian plaster the best, too," he said when she'd finished. "In the light gray. And you do the plastering, too, huh? Because this can't be done with just paint, right?"

"Right. It's actually paint, then a light layer of plaster applied just so, then some sanding and potentially more paint or polishing. And, yes, I can do it all," she assured.

"Did you go to school to learn this stuff?" he asked.

"No. In college I studied art history and conservation. My grandfather was a housepainter, though, so I grew up helping him and learning the basics—and cleaning a lot of paint brushes." She laughed. "The tole painting in the shop and the murals and stenciling and wall finishes sort of combine what I learned in college with what my grandfather taught me. And I do some restoration, too—like the frame on the mirror you saw yesterday."

"So you got a degree in art history and conservation but you didn't want to work as an art historian?"

"There aren't a lot of opportunities in the field—it wasn't the smartest choice in terms of degrees that can be translated into a job. When I graduated from college I went to work for a company that did art restoration but—" She paused, feeling as if she were talking too much. "You don't want to hear this."

"I do, though," he said, sounding genuinely interested. "Did you get to restore paintings or—"

"I was mostly just the gofer—I did a lot of cleaning brushes then, too," she said. "It was a trainee position but I didn't stay long enough to actually get any hands-on experience, so it didn't really do me any good."

"Why didn't you stay long?"

"I quit to get married...." But she didn't want to talk about that so she quickly continued, "Then when I needed to get into the workforce again, I had the degree but no experience, and without any experience the degree was just a dusty piece of paper that didn't do me any good."

"So you opened your own shop."

"Holly and I have been friends since first grade—Holly owns the pet supply store next door—and she talked me into the shop. I came up with the idea of doing outside work, offering services as a restorer and doing jobs like this one—the fancier, more specialized things that my grandfather wouldn't have done as a housepainter."

Cade nodded. "Are you doing okay—financially, I mean?"

Nati laughed. "Are you afraid I'm going to charge you an arm and a leg for this?"

He laughed. "No, I'm just wondering if you're doing okay."

"I don't have a retirement fund. Or savings. But I'm only six months into this and I'm meeting my operating expenses. Arden's city council is putting a lot of resources into getting people into Old Town—there are all kinds of events planned like the Scarecrow Festival. Plus, with the holiday shoppers and word-of-mouth bringing in jobs like this one of yours, I think I'm about where I should be with a new business."

"Well, you *are* pretty far from retirement age so there's time yet for that, but the no-savings part worries me a little."

Nati laughed again. "You're worried about me?"

"Oh, you know… I'm just saying that you should have savings…."

"Believe me, it's one of my goals. But for now, I like what I'm doing and I feel good about it, so I'm okay with things. And as for charging you an arm and a leg—you'll pay for the materials and my labor will be my standard by-the-hour fee. You can check with whoever it was who recommended me and you'll find out that I charged them exactly the same rate. For this job…"

She did some computations and then passed him her figures.

"…this is my ballpark bid."

Cade barely glanced at it before he said, "That seems fine to me."

"You can get another bid. Or two or three if you want," she said.

"No, you're who I want—" He cut himself off as if something about that had come out wrong. Then he said, "—for this job. You came highly recommended. And I realize if you get into this and it takes longer than you think, your labor charge will be higher and that's okay, too—I know this is only an estimate, it isn't carved in stone."

"Sooo, we're in business?" Nati asked.

"We are definitely in business," he said, seeming more pleased and enthusiastic about it than he needed to be. He was looking so intently at her that she had the oddest sense that there was something more personal to this than getting his wall fixed.

She told herself that she had to be imagining it, and began to gather her samples.

"Shall I pay you half now, half when the job is finished, or how do you want to work this?" he asked then.

Oh. She'd forgotten about getting paid. Where was her head?

As if she didn't know…

"You can just write me a check for the estimated cost of the materials and we'll settle up the rest when I finish," she said, pretending she hadn't completely overlooked an important detail.

"Let me get my checkbook," he said, leaving the dining room. He was gone only a moment before he returned with checkbook in hand.

While he was writing the check, Nati said, "I'll bring

the formal paperwork with me tomorrow. If I don't see you, I'll leave it for you to sign and then pick it up when I come on Monday. I probably won't see you then, either, because I assume you'll be at work."

And why was she feeling slightly disappointed at the thought that she likely wouldn't encounter him much—if at all—while she was doing this job?

No, she didn't want an answer to that question. She just shooed away the feeling.

"I'm sure I'll be here at various points," he said as if it were a promise, looking into her eyes as he handed her the check. "But for now I've probably kept you longer than I should have—I know it's Friday night and you must have a date or something planned with your…husband?"

She'd told him she'd quit her first job out of college to get married. She hadn't said anything else about that. Was he as curious about her personal life as she'd been about his? Because that was how it sounded.

"I'm not married anymore. I'm divorced."

"I'm sorry. For long?"

"It was final six months ago, but there was a year before that when it was…in process. And no, there isn't a date, or a fiancé, or a significant other or even a whoever for me, either. But I do have a new bottle of bubble bath waiting for me…."

She stood, holding her materials like school books.

"I guess I'll see you tomorrow or Monday…or maybe I won't," she said as she headed for the front door.

"Tomorrow or Monday," he repeated.

Cade opened the door when they reached it and, as

Nati stepped outside, he peered over her head and said, "Where's your car?"

"I parked on the street."

"Ah..." he said, following her as if he intended to walk her to the curb.

"It's okay, you don't have to come all the way out here," Nati said.

"It's after dark—this neighborhood is relatively safe, but still..."

He had manners. That was nice. He went ahead of her to her car door and waited while she unlocked it, then leaned in to open it for her.

"It sticks," she warned.

But for him it opened just fine.

"From now on go ahead and pull into the driveway," he instructed as she got in behind the wheel. "Use the side closest to the house—I'll use the other side while you're working here so you won't have to carry things as far."

Also nice. And considerate.

Not that that mattered, either. She was just doing a job for him. Here and gone. *Don't get sucked in.*

"Drive safe," he said as he closed her door.

Nati nodded and turned the key in her ignition, willing the aging car to start on the first try since Cade was still standing there, watching her.

Luck was with her, because the engine turned over instantly for once and allowed her to put the car into gear to leave.

But not before she let herself have one last glance at Cade standing there as if he were keeping her safe until she could get on her way. Tall, broad-shouldered and so handsome…

Nati raised a hand in a little wave and finally gave the car enough gas to actually put it into motion.

All the while unable to prevent herself from fantasizing about being back in that big Georgian house again.

And spending the rest of her Friday night alone there with Cade Camden…

Chapter Three

"I brought lunch."

"I'm so glad! I'm starving," Nati told her friend when Holly arrived at the shop around noon on Saturday. "Did you get your errands done?"

"Every one—thanks to you being here to share shop duties now. How was the morning?"

"You made a couple of nice sales. I've only had a few looky-loos, nobody bought anything."

"But now you'll have the money from doing the Camden wall—you were smart not to turn that down."

Nati shrugged, unable to decide whether working for Cade Camden was good or bad. Certainly the money was good. The fact that she was working for a Camden—whom she'd actually had dreams about all night long in which one or more of them was hot and bothered and not entirely clothed—didn't seem like such a good thing.

"What's for lunch?" she asked, changing the subject.

"My throw-everything-in salad with the homemade dressing you like."

"Yum. Thanks for this—I was running late this morning and didn't have time to fix lunch. I was going to skip it," Nati said.

"Another sleepless night because of The Camden?" Holly guessed.

Holly was a childhood friend who was more like a sister to Nati. They'd always told each other everything, so Holly knew that Nati was suffering doubts about having anything to do with a Camden. Holly also knew that Nati had been up half the night after her Thursday meeting with him. But last night? Holly didn't know about last night yet.

"I had trouble falling asleep again and then when I did the dreams I had were… Wow!" she confessed to her friend.

Holly laughed. "Cade Camden is the stuff 'wow' dreams are made of," she concurred.

Holly had come in just as Cade had left on Thursday so she'd seen him.

"Have you decided yet if you're going to tell your grandfather you're working for a Camden?" Holly asked as they ate. Nati's friend had gone to her side of the door that connected their shops.

"No, I still don't know if I should tell him or not," Nati said.

"He gets home tonight?"

Nati's grandfather, Jonah Morrison, was on a brief vacation in Las Vegas with some of his lodge buddies.

"Late tonight. I have until tomorrow to think about it, I guess," Nati answered.

"I think you should tell him. I know you—you'll be sorry if you don't. You'll hate lying—even by omission—and you'll worry that he might find out. And I don't think he'll care, anyway. What went on was a lifetime ago, and your grandfather will be glad you have the work. He'll say good for you for taking some of the Camdens' money."

Holly had grown up across the street from the Morrisons, so she knew Nati's grandfather well.

"Yeah, I could see him saying that," Nati agreed.

"Because he's the sweetest guy in the world. He'd give you the shirt off his back. He's so tenderhearted that he tears up at the sight of puppies and kittens, and he'll just be happy that you have money coming in no matter who it's from."

"Right—it was more like my great-grandparents to rant and rave about the Camdens, not my grandfather."

"Although he might feel guilty *because* you need the work—" Holly cut herself off. "No, forget that. It'll be fine. You need the money, and your grandfather won't care who you're working for. Just do the job, take the check, then wash your hands of the Camdens."

"Yeah," Nati agreed, unsure if she was doing the right thing.

Or if washing Cade Camden out of her thoughts when this was all over with would be as easy as Holly made it sound.

"It's just me..."

Nati heard Cade's voice coming from the entrance as he let himself in. It sent a tiny tingle up her spine.

It was after five o'clock on Saturday and she'd been expecting that he might show up any time. And maybe hoping—just a little—that he would. She couldn't help it.

She was cleaning up the remnants of the mess made from tearing off wallpaper, cleaning the wall and then priming it, when Cade came into the dining room.

Apparently working on Saturday didn't require him to dress up because he was wearing a pale yellow sport shirt tucked into a pair of jeans. A pair of jeans that he wore to perfection slung slightly low on his hips. Nati's jaw dropped for a split second before she forced her eyes up to his face, which looked remarkably sexy with a five-o'clock shadow.

"Hi," she said, her voice catching in her throat.

"Hi. I'm so glad you're still here."

She didn't know why he should be glad but his words gave her a wave of satisfaction anyway.

"Five minutes later and I wouldn't have been," she informed him as she stuffed the last sheet of wallpaper into the trash bag she'd brought with her. "The contract is there on the dining room table," she added with a nod in that direction. "I was just going to leave it for you."

"Any chance you could stick around for a while? I can sign the contract and then there's another job I'm hoping you might take. If you don't have to be anywhere in a hurry maybe we could talk about it…"

"No, I don't have to be anywhere—in a hurry or otherwise," she said, realizing only after the fact that it made her sound like a dud.

But what difference did it make if he knew her social life was nearly nonexistent? In fact, it was better that he think she was a dud, she told herself. Maybe it would act to deter any interest in her.

As she pulled the drawstring closed on the trash bag, she said, "I'll take this to my car and give you a minute to read the contract, then come back."

"Okay," Cade said with more enthusiasm than seemed warranted.

Outside the sun had gone down and taken the warm autumn temperature with it, so after putting the trash bag into her trunk Nati opened her car door to retrieve the overblouse she'd brought with her.

Slipping it on, she tried not to think about the fact that while she'd worn a perfectly work-appropriate beige crewneck T-shirt and jeans, the overblouse took the outfit beyond work clothes and made it a tad dressier. It was fine-gauge wool in deep cocoa brown, with long sleeves and an asymmetrical front opening that fastened at her hip with one large button.

Yes, it added another layer and a bit more warmth, but just a bit. Its primary purpose was to spruce her up a little. Which was what had been in the back of her mind when she'd brought it with her.

And when she took a brush from her glove compartment, ran it through her hair, and then applied some lip gloss, it was hard to deny her intentions—she wanted to look her best now that Cade Camden was home.

But only because she wanted to be presentable when dealing with a client…

She called herself a liar and went back inside.

She hoped Cade wouldn't notice that she'd done anything. But he glanced at her the minute she rejoined him in the dining room, giving her a quick once-over.

He seemed to approve, though, because the faintest of appreciative smiles brushed across his lips before he handed her the signed contract.

"That was quick," she said with raised eyebrows. "You didn't have any questions or problems with it?"

"Nope, looks just right to me," he said, almost as if he was commenting more on her appearance than on the contract.

Then he switched his attention to the wall she'd spent the afternoon working on.

"This is already an improvement," he observed.

"It's only primed but just losing that gaudy wallpaper was a big step."

"Did you have any problems with it?"

"Only in a few spots. Nothing big. And I got everything off without doing any damage, so I think we're good to go from here."

"I told my grandmother about what you did with the frame on that mirror I saw in your shop and it reminded her that she has *her* grandmother's hope chest."

"That would be your great-great-grandmother's hope chest. How old is that?"

"GiGi—that's what we call my grandma—is seventy-five. If we stick with round numbers, let's say GiGi's mother would have been twenty years older than her, add another twenty years to get GiGi's grandmother's age, so the hope chest has to be..." He laughed. "*Really* old."

Nati laughed, too, at his failure to come up with a precise number.

"I'd never seen it before," he went on, "but GiGi made me root around in the attic until I found it this morning. It's kind of like a wooden steamer trunk. The overall finish has survived pretty well, but the design painted on the front, around the latch, and on the very top has faded nearly into oblivion. GiGi wanted me to ask you if you could redo it the way you redid the mirror frame."

"I'd have to check it out to know."

"It's a leafy vine motif with some hearts and flowers—"

"That's the kind of thing I do. But I can't say if the original design is restorable until I see it."

"There are some spots that are gone altogether," he warned. "Especially around the latch—"

"Sure, where hands brushed against it over and over again. But if there's enough of the pattern left in other places I can usually figure out what's missing and fill it in."

"You just have to see it first to know," he repeated. "What about now? If you don't have anywhere to be, we could go over there and take a look..."

"Oh. Now? To your grandmother's house?"

"It doesn't have to be now. We can set it up for later. I just thought that since we're both free, and you're already on this side of town, and GiGi's place is just over on Gaylord—"

Saturday night and he was as free as she was? He didn't have a party or an event or a date with some drop-dead-gorgeous socialite? That was hard to believe.

"Sure, I can do that," she answered after a pause.

"We can take my car or you can follow me over and go home from there—your choice," he offered.

The thought of riding in a car with him seemed a

little awkward and at the same time too appealing, so she said, "I'll just follow you in my car."

"Okay. Then if you're all finished here, why don't we go? We might be just in time for you to meet GiGi before she leaves for her dinner plans."

GiGi. Every time he said it there was affection in his tone. Georgianna Milner Camden. Nati's grandfather's old love.

Nati's curiosity suddenly ran high.

"Okay," she agreed, worrying all over again that this whole thing might smack of disloyalty in some way. But she couldn't stop herself now.

Cade ushered her out the front door and back to her car. It was parked beside his in the driveway.

"Just follow me," he suggested.

"Okay," Nati agreed, hoping her old clunker could keep up with his sleek black sports car.

As they drove the short distance, Nati saw him repeatedly glance into his rearview mirror to make sure she was there. But he drove conservatively enough for her not to have any problem following him.

After a few minutes, Cade turned onto a driveway that ran through the gap in a ruddy redbrick wall bordering an enormous estate.

She followed him up the stone-paved drive and around the fountain that formed the centerpiece of the front grounds. They came to a stop near a five-car garage. It was attached to an expansive house that would have made her former in-laws drool with envy because it dwarfed theirs.

The Tudor mansion curved out from the garage in a two-story semicircle of brick, stucco, wood trim and arched windows. The classically steep roof was dotted with dormers, two sculpted brick chimneys and gables under which thick green ivy grew.

Nati was embarrassed by the sound her car made when she turned off the engine but she pretended not to be when she got out.

"This is beautiful," she said with unveiled awe as Cade led the way up the three steps onto the wide curved landing that stretched out from the house's entrance.

Cade didn't knock on the huge single door with its stained and leaded glass in the upper half. He merely opened it, held it and motioned for Nati to go in ahead of him.

She did, stepping as gingerly as if she were walking on eggshells, into an enormous foyer with a vaulted ceiling and a crystal chandelier centered over a round entry table large enough for a family of six to eat around had it been a dining table.

Cade followed her in, closed the door and shouted, "GiGi? Are you still here?"

"In the den," a voice from somewhere farther into the house shouted back.

Having been married to the heir to an airline fortune, Nati had had the occasion to see some pretty impressive places. But nothing had compared to what she saw as she followed Cade to the left of the foyer, through double doors and into an oak-paneled den where two women were standing at a curio, one of them dusting antique watches, and then handing them to the other woman who carefully placed them on display.

Nati judged the woman replenishing the display to be

about sixty years old—too young to be Cade's grandmother. She was short, plump, with rosy round cheeks. She was dressed casually in knit slacks and a sweatshirt, her ash-blond hair cut close to her head all over in a low-maintenance cap style.

The other woman was older—more the age of Nati's seventy-five-year-old grandfather and more likely to be the matriarch of the Camden clan. Like the sweatshirted woman, she was also not much more than five feet tall and had a somewhat fluffy figure that said she enjoyed her food and robust good health, too. She was the more attractive of the two women, with a lined face that still bore the signs of glowing beauty. Her hair was salt-and-pepper colored, and she wore it short and curly. And despite the fact that she was dressed in a stylish black evening suit with a lacy white blouse and several strands of pearls, she was doing the dusting.

"You're a little overdressed for that, don't you think, GiGi?" Cade teased when he strolled up to her and kissed her cheek. Then, turning to kiss the cheek of the other woman, he said, "Hi, Margaret. What are you doing still cleaning on a Saturday night? And where's Louie?"

"We cleaned this room from top to bottom today," GiGi said, before the other woman could answer. "I have some time while I wait for my ride to dinner tonight, so we're doing this one last thing so we can be done with it. Then Margaret and Louie are going bowling. Without me."

"Tonight's the end of the tournament," Margaret said. "Keep your fingers crossed that we take home the trophy."

"But they're at a disadvantage if I'm not there," GiGi said.

"She's right but I can't talk her out of ditching the dinner."

Nati was at a loss as she looked on. She understood that the dressed-up woman was Georgianna Camden. But who was the other woman? A close enough relative to warrant a hello kiss from Cade, it seemed.

But why were they cleaning? After six years with the Pirfoys, Nati knew that absolutely no one but the staff would have performed a cleaning chore. Certainly her mother-in-law would never have dirtied her hands with a dust cloth, let alone participated in a bowling tournament. And she wouldn't have accepted shouted greetings in *her* house.

Finally Cade turned to Nati and did the introductions. "GiGi, this is Nati Morrison. Nati, my grandmother, Georgianna Camden."

GiGi handed the last of the watches to Margaret and turned her dark blue eyes to Nati.

"Call me GiGi—everyone does. It makes it simpler," she announced.

"And this," Cade added with a nod toward the other woman, "is Margaret Haliburton—she and her husband Louie have been taking care of the house and the rest of us forever. We couldn't make it without them."

"It's nice to meet you both," Nati said.

There was the sound of a car horn honking from out front and the woman in the sweatshirt threw up her hands. "That's Louie—I better go. See you all later," she said. Nati had never seen a housekeeper be so casual with her employers.

Once goodbyes had been said, Georgianna Camden turned to study Nati. "Nati Morrison. And your grandfather is Jonah Morrison, from Northbridge, Montana, Cade tells me."

"He is."

The older woman's eyebrows arched in interest. "So he's still alive and kicking?"

"He is that, too."

"And he is well, I hope?"

"He's doing okay. Enjoying his retirement. He's actually in Las Vegas with some friends right now."

"Good for him!" GiGi laughed and leaned toward Nati to confide, "I'm not sure if you know this or not, but he and I were quite an item when we were young. I was just a girl—barely sixteen when we first got together—but I thought that man was going to marry me. He had the most beautiful thick auburn hair—"

"He still has beautiful thick hair but now it's snow white," Nati said.

"And when he smiled..." Georgianna Camden shook her head and smiled at her recollection. "His eyes just lit up like a delighted little boy. He was so much fun and he was such a nice person—"

"He still is," Nati assured her as her curiosity was stirred.

Her grandfather had always maintained the possibility that Georgianna had had no idea what the Camdens did in driving his family out of town. After hearing her great-grandparents' opinions on the subject, Nati had thought that giving Georgianna the benefit of the doubt was merely big of Jonah. But now, meeting the woman, hearing the things she had to say about Jonah, Nati had to wonder if her grandfather might be right, if maybe the woman hadn't known what went on.

The doorbell rang just then, and GiGi shook her head as if she wasn't thrilled about it. "That must be my ride. As far as I'm concerned these charities shouldn't be spending money on a car and driver to get me to their functions. They should be putting the money to better use. If it weren't a cause I care about I'd tell them to blow it out their ear and I'd go bowling with Margaret and Louie."

"But this way you get to arrive like the Queen of England," Cade teased her.

His grandmother rolled her eyes, then said, "There's shepherd's pie in the fridge. Help yourselves." To Nati she added, "I'm so happy to meet you. I hope you can do something with my old trunk. I'd like to put it at the foot of my bed. Cade has bragged and bragged about what he's seen of your work. And tell Jonah hello for me when you see him."

Nati nodded without committing to that and said, "It was nice to meet you, Mrs.—"

"GiGi—I hate the whole misses stuff," she insisted before she said good-night and left. Nati stared after her, still stunned by the difference between what she'd just seen of Georgianna Camden and her former in-laws.

"And now you've met my grandmother," Cade said, then with a loving laugh, "People will be hearing about that car and driver all night."

"She has a point," Nati said, realizing that she'd liked the elderly woman. Well enough that she found herself wanting to give her the same benefit of the doubt that her grandfather gave.

"So, what do you say? A trip to the attic?" Cade suggested then.

Nati switched gears, reminding herself that despite GiGi's warm treatment, she was there only for work.

"A trip to the attic—are you sure we don't need a car and driver for that?" Nati joked as she glanced around the den, which alone was the size of her entire apartment in her grandfather's basement.

"There *is* an elevator if you don't think you can make it," he goaded.

"I'll give it my best shot but I can't promise."

Cade didn't provide her with a formal tour of the place as he led her up the wide, curving staircase with its carved-oak posts and banister. But as they ascended from the entrance hall to the second floor, Nati caught a glimpse of a formal living room and a formal dining room on the ground level.

Formal, but not stuffy, she thought, surprised by the warm, homey look of the house that was as palatial inside as it was out.

On the second level she counted seven bedrooms. Then Cade took her around an alcove to a set of hidden stairs that were not as fancy as the others, and they climbed to the attic where Cade flipped on the lights.

The steep angle of the roof caused the walls of the attic to slant drastically. But it was still such a large, open space that there was plenty of room for even Cade to stand tall and straight as they stepped into the space, which was cluttered with old furniture and boxes. It was an antique dealer's dream.

"The hope chest is over here." Cade led Nati the

short distance to a stately old steamer trunk with fading decorations.

Nati took a close look at it, then said, "You're right, the chest itself is in remarkably good shape, and there is enough of the design left for me to reproduce it. So this is do-able."

"Then you'll take on this job, too?"

Nati was not in a position to turn down any job. "Sure."

"GiGi will be happy to hear that."

"I'll need to work on it in my shop, though—better lighting so that I can mix and match the colors—"

"I'll get it to you."

Nati laughed. "Strapped to the top of your sports car? I think this might tip it over."

He smiled at her. "Louie has a truck. He'll help get this out of here and I'll bring it to you."

"I have access to a truck, too. If you want, I can—"

"No, I'll get it to you," he said, impressing her with his readiness to make things as easy as possible for her.

"Okay, if you say so," she agreed.

"Looks like we have another deal, then. And now that that's settled—I'm starved. What do you say to taking GiGi up on her offer of that shepherd's pie? She's a fantastic cook."

His grandmother dusted *and* cooked?

That further amazed Nati.

Then there was the allure of extending her time with Cade.

The idea had so much appeal that it was a little alarming. Her mind instantly jumped ahead to sitting alone with him, sharing a meal, talking, laughing, spending the next hour or more with a man she had an inordinate urge to get to know. It would almost seem like having a date with him.

Which she could *not* do!

The rich ARE different! she silently shrieked at herself.

No matter how Cade Camden or his grandmother seemed on the surface, no matter how much nicer and warmer they appeared to be than the Pirfoys, underneath it all, Nati had no doubt that the Camdens and the Pirfoys were in the same camp. To them, she was nothing more than the help.

"Thanks, but I should just get going," she forced herself to say.

"Come on… You said you didn't have any plans. And you have to eat…" he cajoled with a smile that could have won him any dinner partner in the world.

Except Nati.

She held her ground by thinking about how much her marriage, her divorce, had cost her.

"No plans, no," she confirmed, "but I do have some work to do and some phone calls to return and my own dinner slow-cooking at home for me."

She didn't. But it sounded possible.

Cade actually looked disappointed—something else Nati found difficult to believe tonight. But he conceded anyway.

"Let's go down the back stairs to the kitchen at least then, so I can swipe some of the shepherd's pie to take home with me."

"Okay," she agreed.

When they reached the second floor, Cade made a

sharp turn away from the alcove that blocked the staircase from view and they went down another concealed flight of steps that dropped them into a restaurant-sized kitchen.

Despite its size, the kitchen was warm and homey and inviting with its navy-blue-and-white checkered-tile floor, its tarnished brass lighting and plumbing fixtures, and the pristine white cupboards. It reminded Nati of an almost as elaborate home in Cape Cod that she'd once visited with her ex-husband.

"This is a chef's dream," she muttered as she took in the commercial-sized refrigerator, the six-burner gas stove with its built-in grill, the double ovens, the triad of sinks and the expansive island in the center of the room that provided ample workspace.

"Ten little chefs," Cade said. "That's what GiGi called us."

Nati was confused and it must have shown. As Cade opened one side of the gargantuan double-doored refrigerator and took out a container, he explained.

"When I was nine I came to live here with my two brothers, my sister, January, and my six cousins."

Nati had heard more than a fair share of ranting against H.J. and his son Hank Camden from her great-grandparents before their deaths. She'd read the occasional newspaper or magazine article about one or all of the Camdens, but she hadn't kept track of how many of them there were or who they were individually. And when it came to any kind of details or family history, she knew nothing at all.

"Why did you all come to live here?" she asked as he

found a smaller container and a spoon, and returned to the island to dish out some of the shepherd's pie.

His chiseled features sobered into sadness even as he said matter-of-factly, "My parents, my aunt and uncle and my grandfather were all killed in a plane crash that year."

"I'm sorry. I didn't know."

"You would have been just a little kid, too. No surprise that you weren't watching the news or that you wouldn't remember even if you had heard about it. The trip was supposed to be a family vacation for all of the adults. But H.J.—my great-grandfather—hurt his back a couple of days before they were all going to leave. He couldn't make it and GiGi volunteered to stay home and take care of him. If that hadn't happened, everyone would have died and all ten of us would have been orphaned. As it was, with only GiGi and H.J. left, GiGi had us all move in with them."

"Your great-grandfather lived here, too?" Nati asked as she studied Cade's profile, committing to memory every angle of that perfect, masculine bone structure.

"H.J. had moved in with my grandparents after he retired and had a heart attack. Between GiGi and H.J.—and Margaret and Louie—they raised all ten of us. Although it was GiGi who was boss."

"You say that like she was a stern taskmaster," Nati said.

"Oh, GiGi was the worst!" he claimed with another of those loving laughs she'd heard from him earlier, and Nati was glad to see any remnants of sad memories disappear.

Still, she rolled her eyes and repeated facetiously,

"The worst? Uh-huh. What does that mean? That she made you share a nanny instead of having your own?"

"There were nannies before the plane crash, when we lived in our separate homes with our own parents—one for the four of us, one for my six cousins. But when we all came here? GiGi didn't believe in nannies. People should raise their own kids—that's what she said."

"So she took on ten of you without any nannies at all?"

"GiGi could have taken on twenty of us," he said with yet another laugh, this one full of respect and admiration, and Nati got lost for a moment in the lines and creases that animated his face.

Dragging herself out of that split second of reverie, she said, "Of course there was the help of Margaret and Louie—are they household staff?"

"That was how they started out years and years ago, but they've long since become family. They were as much the bosses of us as GiGi and H.J. were."

"And they didn't wait on you?" Nati asked skeptically.

"Oh, no. We were responsible for cleaning up after ourselves. The ten of us shared three rooms. We changed the sheets on our own beds, we put away our own laundry, cleaned our own bathrooms, and if we left anything laying around down here, it disappeared forever, no matter how important it was. GiGi raised us the way she was raised and that was all there was to it."

"And you were ten little chefs, too?" Nati asked.

"We were. Meals around here were a very big deal," he assured her. "GiGi and Margaret made breakfast and sometimes lunch. We all ate together—"

"Margaret and Louie, too?"

"Sure. I told you, Margaret and Louie are family."

The Pirfoys would be appalled....

"But dinnertime," Cade continued, "was a time for Margaret and Louie to be alone and for the ten of us and GiGi to meet here in this kitchen every single day to fix dinner. Then we sat down at that table over there—" he pointed to a breakfast nook large enough to seat a football team "—and we ate as a family. GiGi said it was like a farmhouse kitchen. All of us were here, every night, unless someone had a good excuse and GiGi's permission to be somewhere else. We all did the cleanup, too. We still have Sunday dinner here every week, in the formal dining room. Now we don't have to make the meal ourselves. We do have to bring a dish, though...."

"The Camden family *formal* Sunday dinner is potluck?"

"GiGi does the main course and a few other things if the mood strikes her," he confirmed. "But we're responsible for the rest. We don't have to cook the dish ourselves, we can get takeout. Most of us will bring something from one of our favorite restaurants. But yeah, I guess you could say Sunday dinners are sort of potluck."

He closed both the food containers and returned the main one to the refrigerator, turning his back to Nati.

Whose eyes devoured the sight of his broad shoulders. Of his narrow waist. Of that delicious-looking derriere.

Until she yanked them away and said, "The Camdens

were raised on farmhouse dinners and potluck—who would have thought *that!*"

"Has your grandfather ever taken you to his hometown?" Cade asked.

"Northbridge? No, actually I've never been to Montana at all."

"Well, it's a small town through and through. And GiGi always says that you can take the girl out of the small town, but you can't take the small town out of the girl. So we might have lived right here in the heart of Denver—"

"In a mansion," Nati pointed out.

"But we were raised like small-town kids with small-town rules and values. We were taught to take care of each other, of our own, to keep a united front, and to do what was right. GiGi insisted—insists—that every one of us always, always do what's right...."

Nati didn't comment on that. On its face it sounded good. But she'd had her own experience with people who closed ranks and protected themselves and their own assets above all else, and she recognized that what Cade had just said could boil down to that. In fact she thought it was likely. And that kind of a united front could be formidable. Formidable and definitely something she didn't want to have to deal with.

Which was why she took a deep breath and said, "Now that you have your shepherd's pie I really should get going..."

Cade raised the container. "I took enough for two... Last chance—you can follow me home and still have dinner..."

"Can't," she said glibly before she was any more tempted to accept the offer she so wanted to accept.

"Okay, your loss..." he responded just as glibly.

But Nati thought that there might have been a little disappointment to the resigned smile on those supple-looking lips.

Then he sighed, shrugged in defeat and said, "I guess we better go then."

"I don't know the way so I'll follow you."

Container in hand, Cade ushered her out of the kitchen through a doorway that put them in the entry hall directly opposite the front door behind the sweeping staircase.

After letting them both out, he made sure the door was locked then pushed a button on something attached to his key ring and apparently activated an alarm system before he walked Nati to the driver's-side door of her car.

"So what are you bringing to Sunday dinner tomorrow?" she asked as she unlocked her door. She had to jiggle it a little before it finally opened.

"Loaves of bread from an Italian restaurant and bakery I found on the way home from your shop, actually. Want to come?"

That surprised Nati so much she wasn't sure she'd heard him correctly. Or maybe she'd misunderstood him and he *hadn't* just invited her to the Camden's Sunday dinner.

Except then he said, "We're all free to bring anyone we'd like to Sunday dinners. What do you say? Want to meet the whole crew?"

Why was that tempting, too?

Curiosity, Nati decided.

Plus it would mean she'd get to see him.

"No, thanks," she said quickly so she wouldn't accidentally give in to either her curiosity or the yen to be with him. "I'm cooking for my grandfather tomorrow night. But I'll be back at work on your wall on Monday. My friend Holly is watching both shops until three when I'll need to relieve her, but until then I'll be doing the first coat of your paint."

"Okay."

Nati told herself she was imagining things, but for a moment they merely stood there in the lee of her open car door—her looking up into his handsome face, him gazing down at her through those amazing blue eyes—and it was as if she were waiting for him to kiss her good-night.

Which was totally insane, she told herself.

But that didn't stop her from wondering what it might be like if he did just come in a little closer, bend down and press his lips to hers…

No, it *was* insane, she told herself. There was not going to be any kissing between her and Cade Camden. Not now, not ever. Not for any reason. Never.

She finally did break the bonds of that glance and get into her car, reaching for the armrest to close the door.

But Cade was in the way. He leaned on the doorframe, studying her. Looking for all the world as if he might not want her to go.

But that was even more insane.

When he finally stepped out of the way so she could close her door, she said an offhand, "See you next week," and pulled it shut.

"Drive safe," he called through the window, remaining where he was as if he intended to watch her go before he got into his own car.

Nati pulled around his sports car where it was parked just ahead of her, circled the fountain and went down the drive to the street, heading for home.

But not without mentally reading herself the riot act for having even entertained the smallest, briefest thought of kissing Cade Camden.

And even worse, for feeling the slightest disappointment that he hadn't kissed her.

The slightest disappointment that wasn't really slight at all…

Chapter Four

"I'm glad you went and had a good time," Nati said to her grandfather as they discussed his Vegas trip over a spaghetti dinner the next night.

She cut them each a piece of the cake she'd baked, brought the plate to the kitchen table where she'd eaten more meals in her life than she could count, and then ventured tentatively into the subject she was dreading.

"I have something I need to tell you that I'm not sure you're going to like."

"It isn't that you're going back to Doug, is it?" Jonah Morrison said as if that were the worst thing she could possibly say.

"No!" Nati answered with her own revulsion at that idea. "I would never go back to Doug, or Philadelphia, or any of that. I'm here to stay—so don't go looking for some merry widow to move into my place downstairs," she joked.

"No merry widows for me!" Jonah joked in return.

He wasn't a tall man—barely five feet eight—but he was solidly built and still handsome with his shock of thick white hair. In the local senior community he was in high demand by the ladies, so the merry widow jokes were common between them.

"What's going on?" he asked in a more serious tone.

"I've contracted some work with two of the Camdens," Nati said without beating around the bush, deciding it was best to just get to the point.

Her grandfather frowned a little. "Doing…"

"I'm texturing a wall for Cade Camden—he's one of the grandchildren but I don't know where he is in the mix, apparently there are—"

"Ten of them."

So Jonah had kept track.

Nati didn't say anything to that. She merely went on. "And now I'm also going to redo a design on an antique hope chest for Cade's grandmother…."

"Georgianna?"

"I actually met her yesterday…"

"How is she?" Jonah asked without any hint of animosity in his voice.

"Good, I think. She looks good. We didn't really talk about her health but she seems robust. She said to tell you hello."

"She always was a good gal."

Of all the reactions Nati had anticipated, this wasn't one of them. She hadn't expected her grandfather to act as if he were merely hearing about an old acquaintance.

"But she's a Camden," Nati reminded him, wondering if her grandfather had somehow lost sight of that.

"I take some of the blame for that—for her being a Camden," Jonah said, surprising Nati.

"Why would you be to blame for that?" she asked.

"Oh, you know, Nati, I was a young buck back when I knew her. I loved Georgianna, she was something special. But we were just getting out of high school and she wanted to get married—like most girls then. I was full of myself and feeling my oats and I didn't want to be tied down. Not at eighteen. Even to her. So I broke up with her."

"You did? I never knew that. For some reason, I thought she'd dumped you. For the Camden guy."

"No, it was me who did the *dumping,* as you put it," he said with a hint of genuine guilt in his tone. "Hank Camden came along later, at the end of the summer. I was already juggling two other girls by then."

"I've always gotten the impression that H. J. Camden bought the mortgage on your parents' farm and foreclosed on it to get you out of the way so his son could have Georgianna."

The elderly man shrugged. "You got that impression because that's what my folks thought—and yes, I believe old H.J. was worried that Georgianna was carrying a torch for me. I just don't know that Georgianna *was* carrying a torch for me. I do—and did—know that I was no threat to H.J.'s son Hank because I didn't have any intention of starting up again with Georgianna. I'd ended things with her so I was out of the picture. But there was something H.J. said when he came by the farm just as I was helping my father close it up that made me think twice—"

The grimace on her grandfather's lined brow showed more of his guilty feelings.

"He sort of grumbled as I passed by him with the last of our things—something about how now I'd be out of the way and I'd better stay out of the way. It did make me wonder if the old coot had done what he'd done just to get rid of me."

"Would he stoop that low?"

"H. J. Camden? I wouldn't put anything past him. He was a ruthless bugger who made enemies of a lot of people. My dad always said that plane crash was meant for him—"

"The plane crash that killed his son and grandsons and their wives? I just heard about that last night."

"Oh, it was all over the news and in the papers when it happened. The crash killed Hank and both of her sons," Jonah confirmed. "There's always been the suspicion that there was foul play, that something was done to that plane to cause it to crash. But it was never proven. There wasn't enough left to prove anything. But what old H.J. did to my folks and me? That was a drop in the bucket compared to what he did to other people. If you think my folks hated the Camdens, you haven't seen anything!"

"But you? How do you feel about them? I mean, I've never thought that you liked them, but—"

"I don't have any fond memories of H.J., that's for sure—it was a low-down thing he did foreclosing on us. But when it comes to Georgianna? She's just a Camden by marriage. I'd bet my last nickel that she didn't know what her father-in-law was up to with our farm. I never held that against her. In a way, it was more my fault than hers, anyway. If I'd have married her, she wouldn't have gotten together with Hank and the Camdens would have left us alone."

"And then you both ended up in Denver," Nati mused.

"That's not so strange. Two of my lodge brothers are from Montana, too, and came here for the same reason my family did—the advantages of a bigger city where there's still the feel of the West, where there's still the mountains and pretty much the same weather and like-minded people who don't think wearing a pair of cowboy boots makes you a hick."

"But all these years both you and your old girlfriend have lived in the same city, and you've never had any kind of contact?"

"No," Jonah said as if the idea were farfetched. "There was no reason we would. It's not like we ran in the same circles—a housepainter and the mama bear of the high-and-mighty Camdens. The only way we would have ever run into each other is if I'd have been hired to paint her house and I'm sure old H.J. wouldn't have let *that* happen. Not that I would have taken the job…"

"But it's all right with you that I work for them?" Nati asked.

"There's no history between you and them. And their money is as good as anyone else's," Jonah said.

"So you don't mind?"

"Honey, after all you've done for me, all you did for your gramma, and ending up where you've ended up because of it? How could I begrudge you making your living wherever you need to? Just don't take any guff from any of them."

Nati laughed and instantly thought of the warmth

of Cade's smile, the consideration he'd already shown her, how easy it was to be with him. "So far there's no guff for me to take."

"Which one of them did you say you were working for again?"

"Cade. Georgianna is his grandmother. Apparently all the grandkids call her GiGi."

"Well, I hope they all took after her rather than the other side of the family."

"I don't know. I do know that he has her blue eyes."

"She did have the most beautiful blue eyes!" Jonah reminisced.

And just that quick the image of Cade's eyes, of his entire face popped into Nati's mind and sent something tingling all through her.

But all she said was, "So does her grandson."

And yet it was enough to cause her grandfather's brows to arch in surprise before she changed the subject by asking how he liked the cake.

Nati spent Monday morning putting the first coat of paint on Cade's wall and then returned to her shop for the remainder of the day without crossing paths with the man himself.

Although she couldn't shake the disappointment she felt over not getting to see him, she had a firm talk with herself on the drive to her shop about how it was for the best, about how there was absolutely no reason for her to be giving him a second thought.

But by the end of her workday he was still on her mind and the fact that she hadn't been with him since Saturday evening felt to her like an eternity.

Then, minutes from closing up the store, she looked out her front window and caught sight of a truck going by. Driven by Cade.

Okay, so it was totally ridiculous and uncalled for that she ran around her checkout counter and craned to watch the truck turn the corner and pull into the small four-space parking lot behind the store.

But that's what she did. Excitement ran through her like a sudden chill. Her eyes hadn't been playing tricks on her—it really was Cade behind that wheel.

Her very next thought was that she'd been working all day and she had no idea how she looked.

So she ran like a rabbit for the bathroom she shared with Holly.

In the mirror above the sink she saw that her hair was a tad flat, but her mascara and blush were okay. Her jeans were paint-free. She hadn't put on the gray shirt she was wearing over a white tank top until after she'd finished painting Cade's wall, so that was clean and continued to be wrinkle-free.

If only she could get to her purse and run a brush through her hair and put on some lip gloss…

Another dash took her out of the bathroom and behind her counter again. Keeping an eye on the front of her store to make sure there was no sign of Cade yet, she unlocked the cupboard where she stowed her purse, whipped it out and nearly threw things from inside of it in her search for her hairbrush and lip gloss. Finally finding them, she used both in a hurry, telling herself the whole time that she was acting like some kind of crazed teenager.

Popping a mint into her mouth and jamming her

purse back into its cubby, she straightened up from behind the counter just in time to find Cade coming in her front door. He was wielding a dolly with his grandmother's hope chest strapped to it.

"Good, I made it before you closed!" he said as he pushed open the door with that oh-so-fine rear end of his and rolled the dolly into the store.

"Let me help you," Nati said, realizing only belatedly that she should have at least opened the door for him.

He wheeled the chest into the center of the shop and set the dolly upright, keeping it steady with one hand. He turned to smile at her as if he just might be as happy to see her as she was to see him.

"Hi," he finally said.

"Hi," Nati responded, attempting but failing to contain the grin she could feel on her face.

"I told you I'd get this thing to you," he said. "I probably should have called to say I was coming but I got busy. Then there was a lot of traffic and I accidentally left my cell phone in my car when I switched to the truck at GiGi's, so I still couldn't call. I was afraid I'd get here and find you gone for the day."

"Another ten minutes and you would have."

"I'm glad it didn't take another ten minutes, then. Where do you want it?" he asked with a nod at the hope chest.

"I have a workroom in back," Nati answered, pointing over her shoulder with her thumb.

"Lead the way."

She did, ordering herself to calm down, reminding herself that this was only business.

She opened the door for him to go through and said, "Just set it in the middle of the room."

Cade maneuvered the dolly between worktables cluttered with other projects in various stages of completion. He put the hope chest where she'd told him to and unstrapped it from the dolly.

"There you go—she's all yours," he announced.

"Thanks for playing delivery boy."

"Want to hire me?" he joked.

"Are you looking for new employment?" she countered.

"You never know..."

They both laughed at the absurdity of that.

"The wall looks good—I went home at lunch and saw it. I thought I might catch you but you'd been there and gone."

"That's just the base color, it will get darker as I go along—in case you're worried. I know it looks a little bright at this stage."

"I trust you," he said.

Now what? Nati wondered. He'd brought the hope chest, they'd talked about the progress on the wall, he'd probably just leave.

But she so didn't want that!

So she said, "How was Sunday dinner with the family yesterday?"

"Same as all the Sunday dinners—good. That's what keeps us coming back," he joked again. "How was your dinner with your grandfather?"

"That was good, too. I always like spending time with him."

"What about tonight? You have plans?" Cade asked, as smoothly as if they were old friends.

"No…" Nati said tentatively, unsure why he was asking.

"I skipped lunch to go home to see you—and wasn't smart enough to fix myself something to eat while I was there. So I'm starving. How's that little grill pub across the street?"

Nati's shop was among the six blocks of suburban Arden's historic buildings that had been remodeled in an attempt to gentrify the area. After years of deterioration that had left the neighborhood with nothing but vacant storefronts and antique shops that were more like dumping grounds for garage-sale rejects, it was getting a new life.

The update had brought in many small businesses and new restaurants that were all doing their best to promote and support each other.

"They serve fantastic burgers and the best fish and chips I've ever eaten. And their sticky chocolate-toffee pudding is too fantastic to pass up for dessert."

"Then I don't think we should."

"We?" Nati echoed.

"I hate eating alone. And if you don't have plans, why don't you let me buy you dinner? And sticky chocolate-toffee pudding for dessert."

Of course she shouldn't say yes, Nati knew that. She'd spent two days fighting against the attraction she had for this guy by reminding herself of all the reasons he was well-dressed poison to her, and of the fact that she was only six months out of her marriage and was barely getting her head above water again anyway.

And yet *no* was not what she heard come out of her mouth….

"I guess I could keep you company."

Cade's grin got even bigger. "Music to my ears," he said. "You do whatever you have to do to close up. I'll put Louie's dolly in the truck and meet you back here."

Nati only had to turn off lights to finish closing up but she used a few minutes to try to get herself under control. To put things into perspective.

Dinner. You can have dinner with him, but that's it, she told herself. *And you'd better spend the whole time finding things wrong with him. For a change.*

With that goal in mind, Nati took her purse, turned off the lights and met Cade out front.

Reprimanding herself along the way for how excited she was to be spending the next hour or so with him…

"Tell me about this grandfather of yours," Cade suggested after they'd ordered—a hamburger for him, fish and chips for Nati. "GiGi seems to think pretty highly of him—she says he's a *wonderful* man…"

"My grandfather is terrific. He loves life, he's always cheery, he's generous and kind and sweet and—"

"A little like his granddaughter?" Cade muttered with a small smile.

"I wish I was more like my grandfather—I adore him," Nati said, pretending not to hear the compliment in Cade's words even though it pleased her to no end.

"The more my grandmother talks about him, the more I think she might have felt that way about him, too," Cade said.

"Until *your* grandfather happened along?"

"That makes it sound like my grandfather stole her away from yours, but if I've got the timeline right, GiGi and your grandfather had split up before my grandfather even met her."

Did he also know that Jonah had dumped GiGi?

Nati thought it was better not to venture into that territory. "Hard to know what all went on so many years ago," Nati said softly.

"How did your grandfather meet *your* grandmother…?" Cade asked, just as their food arrived.

"You want the whole family history?" Nati asked with a laugh.

"Sure."

And he actually seemed interested.

But she also knew from experience that her humble beginnings could be a big turn-off for rich boys like Cade. Which might be a good thing if she wanted to keep her distance. So she said, "My grandfather met my grandmother here, in Denver. About five years after his family moved from Northbridge. He was a housepainter by profession and she worked in a hardware store selling paint."

"Very romantic," Cade teased. "And they had how many kids?"

"Just my father."

"One kid? That's unheard of in my family," he joked. "Was that because they only wanted one kid or because they couldn't afford more or…?"

"More just didn't happen," Nati said, repeating what her grandmother had always told her.

"And from one son came you."

"Also an only child," Nati confirmed.

His eyebrows arched over those blue, blue eyes as he ate a bite of burger.

Then he said, "You're from a small family. Was that how your parents wanted it or was it another act of nature or was it economics...?"

"Economics?" Nati repeated.

"What does your dad do for a living?" Cade persisted.

Nati drenched a morsel of fried cod in vinegar and salt, ate it and then said, "My dad doesn't do anything for a living now because he isn't living—he and my mother were killed in a highway accident when I was thirteen."

"Oh. I'm sorry. I didn't know."

"No reason that you would have," Nati said before she went on to answer Cade's question about what her father had done for a living. "Both of my parents had a lot of jobs until I was four—nothing worked out for them, they hated nine-to-five, weren't good at taking orders. Then they discovered big-rig truck driving."

Cade's eyebrows went up slightly again. Nati had expected more than that but decided he was just too polite to respond with the same level of horror that her in-laws had.

"That's right, both my mother and my father were truckers," she said, watching to see if that could drain the color out of his face the way it had blanched it from her mother-in-law's when she'd heard it.

Cade ate a couple of French fries before he said, "Truck driving is an honest living. Did your parents like doing it?"

"It was a way of making money. The two of them

were restless spirits who found each other and then found a way to make a living out of that restlessness."

"Do you think things would have turned out differently if your family had stayed in Northbridge? My grandmother said they owned a farm there—do you think your father would have been happier working outside?"

It suddenly occurred to Nati that Cade knew what his great-grandfather had done to her family. And if he knew, then didn't that mean that his grandmother knew? Maybe Georgianna Camden *didn't* deserve the benefit of the doubt.

On the other hand, this conversation suddenly gave her the sense that he might be carrying around some sort of guilt or shame, or at the very least that he didn't approve of what his great-grandfather had done and was looking for reassurance of some kind.

Nati had no idea why she had that feeling. And even though she was curious about it, the history between their families didn't seem like something to get into. Especially not with a client.

And to her, Cade *was* only a client, she reminded herself.

Even if he was also mouth-wateringly good-looking and extremely pleasant company. Even if he did make the woman in her more aware of his pure masculinity than she wanted to be. Even if this whole thing did seem like a nice dinner date and she couldn't for the life of her find anything at all wrong with Cade…

After thinking a moment, she answered his question about her father.

"I guess he might have liked working in the open

air. Having to sit behind a desk, going to meetings he thought were stupid, having a boss standing behind him cracking the whip—those are the things he hated about his jobs before he became a trucker. But my parents loved the open road, seeing different places, not being tied down, so I can't really say if they would have been happy as farmers. And they probably wouldn't have met at all if the family had stayed in Northbridge. My mom was from Denver. Actually, now that I think about it, so was my grandmother, so she and my grandfather wouldn't have met, either—the whole course of things would have been different."

"But ultimately you think that truck driving worked out for your parents?" Cade asked as if he wanted to believe that.

"As well as anything."

"And what about you? Were you raised on the road?"

"I was essentially raised by my grandparents," Nati said as she finished her fish, ate one more fry and then pushed her plate away.

"Like me, except your parents were still alive?" he asked, finishing his meal, too, and motioning to their waitress that they were ready for dessert.

"My mother was seven years younger than my father. She was only nineteen when I was born," Nati explained. "She and my father were married, but motherhood? That wasn't for her. With all the job changes and income instability, my father hadn't ever moved out of my grandparents' place, then he married my mother and moved her in, too. So that's where they brought me home to when I was born and that's still where we were living when my parents took up over-the-road truck driving as a team."

"And left you with your grandparents?"

"I'd go with my parents occasionally but not for really long hauls. If it was a short run and I was on vacation from school, sometimes they'd take me, but not too often. Everyone agreed that a child should have stability and being at home with my grandparents provided that."

"How did you feel about that?"

The sticky chocolate-toffee pudding they'd agreed to share arrived with two spoons. The waitress removed their dinner plates and set it in the middle of the table. When she left, Cade and Nati leaned closer toward each other—and the pudding—to taste it.

Cade took a deep breath, closed his glorious blue eyes and groaned his pleasure after his first bite of the warm chocolate pudding sodden with caramel sauce.

And Nati's mind went somewhere it definitely shouldn't have gone when she wondered if there were other things that elicited a similar response from him.

She took a drink of water to cool off, then tried to distract herself by focusing on the conversation.

"There were times before my parents died that I resented that they weren't there for me," she admitted. "But I loved being with my grandparents. They gave me a good life—spoiled me rotten, to tell you the truth. And it was just the way things were. I guess in some ways it was probably easier on me when my mom and dad died than it was on you because I didn't have to leave my home and go somewhere different to live, with people I wasn't already used to living with. I suffered the loss, but not much of a change in my day-to-day routine."

"I can't imagine that it was much easier," Cade said. "For any of you. Your grandfather probably thought that if you'd all still been in Northbridge on the farm that he might not have lost his only son...."

That thought seemed to trouble Cade but their discussion was cut short when the waitress came to their table and told them that Monday was early-closing night and she needed to settle their bill.

Cade paid with a credit card, denying Nati's offer to pay her own way or even to leave the tip.

They'd finished the pudding by the time the waitress came back with Cade's card and receipt, so they left the restaurant to walk the short distance back to Nati's store. She paused by the door rather than going to the parking lot with him.

"I want to take a look at the hope chest," she said in explanation. "I can probably do some sketches of the design and some color samples to make sure that the restoration isn't brighter or louder than your grandmother may want it. Then you can show it all to her for her approval before I get to work."

"Will you be at the house tomorrow?"

"In the afternoon—I'm watching Holly's shop in the morning, then she's trading places with me at noon. If I finish the sketches and samples tonight I'll bring them with me and leave them on your dining room table."

"But you know, you don't have to work nights to get it done—there really isn't any hurry."

"I know. But I like the peace and quiet, and I'm always anxious to get a new project started." And she was too wound up after being with him—and certainly *not* finding anything wrong with him—to merely go home.

So she thought that she might as well put some of that pent-up energy to good use.

Cade nodded, clearly accepting what she said at face value and having no idea what was behind it. But he didn't move to leave, remaining there on the sidewalk outside of her shop, looking at her as if he needed to memorize her features.

Then he said, "This was nice—thanks for going with me and saving me from dinner alone."

"Sure. Thanks for buying dinner," Nati responded.

He continued to study her.

Nati wasn't sure what he was doing, why he didn't say good-night and go.

Then he reached for her upper arm in a friendly sort of gesture, and said, "Sometimes it's funny how hard it is to just have a meal and some conversation that you really enjoy."

And he leaned forward and kissed her temple.

Nati was so distracted by the glittery sensation of having his hand on her arm that she completely missed the approach of the kiss.

But the warmth of his lips pressed to her skin registered enough to set off even more glittery feelings that cascaded all through her.

She didn't know what to do, though. It seemed as if she should tell him to back off because, along with even bigger issues, he was a client, and their families had bad blood between them.

But at the same time it *had* only been a little kiss on the forehead. And she could well be reading too much into it.

So she didn't say anything at all and instead stood there wondering if she looked as stunned as she felt.

"See you," he said then, giving her arm another light squeeze before he let go of it.

"See you," Nati echoed dimly.

Then she turned to unlock her shop door as he headed to the parking lot.

But as her shaky fingers mishandled the lock, Nati watched him go without seeming to, taking in that rear view that was almost as good as the front. And all she could think was that he *had* kissed her.

And even if it was only on the forehead, she'd seen him kiss his grandmother and the housekeeper, and there was something different about the kiss he'd just given her. Something that wasn't perfunctory or schoolboyish or merely friendly.

It had been enough of a kiss to set her aglow.

Enough of a kiss to leave her at odds with herself when a voice in her head shrieked, "No!"

And the rest of her whispered, "More...."

Chapter Five

"I have Caesar salad, ravioli, pasta puttanesca, some kind of weird little crackers with a bunch of seeds on them, crusty bread and rum-drenched tiramisu—I couldn't make up my mind and got it all, so say you'll stay for dinner."

Those were the words Nati heard immediately following the sound of Cade's front door opening and closing as she was cleaning up her work things for the day.

As promised, she'd spent Tuesday morning watching her shop and Holly's, then come to Cade's house for the afternoon.

"Hi," he greeted her once he arrived in the dining room, bearing a large brown bag.

"Hi," Nati responded with eyebrows raised.

"Did you hear me?" Cade asked, a hopeful and mischievous smile on his divine face.

"You have takeout," Nati said.

"Not *just* takeout—food from this great little mom-and-pop Italian place near here. Enough for two—or three or four," he said. "Interested?"

Much, much *too* interested.

In the man himself, dressed in a charcoal-colored suit, white shirt and a paisley tie that he'd loosened to accommodate an open collar button.

And in the chance to have dinner with him. Again.

Dinner last night *and* tonight? What was up with that? Surely the gorgeous Cade Camden was not some lonely guy desperate for female company. And yet she had the chance at two nights in a row with him.

"Did you get stood up?"

He laughed. "No. I actually cut a meeting short so I could pick up the food and get here before you left. I wanted you to have a little dinner before you make the drive back to the 'burbs."

But still, why? Nati wondered.

Was this just the way the Camdens liked to treat the help?

They *had* made his grandmother's house staff part of the family, she reasoned. Maybe it was merely a bonus they threw in for working for them.

Nati had worked for other people who had offered similar perks. One lady had baked her cookies every day she'd worked on her nursery mural. Some people were just nice that way. She wouldn't have guessed that the almighty Camdens would be among them, but she supposed it was possible.

Just as it was possible that kiss on the temple last night hadn't meant anything, either.

"What do you say? Will you stay and eat or is there

somewhere else you have to be?" Cade asked when she was lost in thought for longer than she probably should have been over such a simple offer.

"There's nowhere else I have to be." And because there was nowhere else she *wanted* to be, she knew she should say no and leave right that minute, so she held up her plaster-spattered hands and said, "But I'm kind of grungy from work."

"Come on, I'll show you the guest bathroom upstairs and you can wash up while I get out of these work clothes. Then I'll meet you in the kitchen—we'll do it casual, sitting on the stools at the island. What do you say?"

It struck her as odd for him to seem so eager for her to say yes.

But rather than speak her mind, Nati said, "Okay, if you don't have anything better to do tonight."

"The governor's ball wouldn't be better," he assured her as he led her from the dining room.

Nati snatched her purse to take with her on the way out.

Despite her curiosity about the rest of the house and how Cade lived, Nati had refrained from snooping. She hadn't been upstairs at all.

The master bedroom was on the second floor, directly across from the top of the stairs, and since the door was open she could see into it. She couldn't help noticing the clothes on the floor and the unmade bed.

From beside her Cade stretched an arm across her shoulders and pivoted her sharply to the right.

"Okay, yeah, I'm not always good about picking up after myself or making the bed. The lady who cleans for me changes the sheets every week and I usually make it on the weekends, but workdays are another story."

He ushered her into the guest room. A room that was perfectly neat and clean, with its queen-size bed nicely made.

"Make yourself at home and I'll see you downstairs."

Nati went into the room, closed the door and found a full-length mirror on the back of it.

She'd worn a smock over her clothes while she'd applied the first layer of decorative plaster to the wall so her jeans and black crewneck sweater were clean. She rolled down the sleeves of the sweater and the white blouse she had on underneath it, then turned the French cuffs of the blouse back over the cuffs of the sweater sleeves.

As she tugged at the blouse collar to make it neater, she noted that the outfit looked a little puritanical but that was probably all the better. An outward appearance of stiffness and standoffishness seemed like a good cover for the fact that underneath it all she was thrilled with the prospect of another evening with Cade.

Clothes under control, she took her hairbrush from her purse, leaned forward and gave her hair a good brushing before she straightened up and let the gold-streaked brown locks fall naturally around her face. Then she pinched her cheeks to add some color, ran her index fingers under her eyelashes to give them a bit of upsweep, and applied fresh lip gloss.

That was about all she could do with what she had in her purse but she judged herself presentable and poked her head back out the bedroom door.

Cade was nowhere in sight and his bedroom door

was closed, but she could hear a shower running. He'd told her to meet him downstairs, so that was where she went.

While she waited, she finished packing up her work things and returned them to her car trunk. Cade was just coming down the stairs when she came back inside.

He was freshly showered, and shaved, and smelled of that cologne she liked so well. He was dressed in a pair of well-aged jeans and a plain white V-neck T-shirt with the long sleeves pushed to his elbows, leaving him looking appealingly casual and relaxed and as if he were ready to settle in for an evening at home. An evening that he'd made sure included her.

But Nati couldn't let that go to her head.

"You weren't trying to sneak away, were you?" Cade asked.

"No, I just put my buckets in the trunk."

"Then work really is done for the day and we can eat!" he said, ushering her toward the kitchen.

"What would you like to drink?" he asked, pointing to one of the tall leather-and-chrome bar stools on the side of the granite-countered island where they were going to eat. "I have wine, soda, iced tea, water—sparkling and otherwise—and orange juice."

Nati made a face. "*Not* orange juice. Or wine since I have to drive home. Maybe sparkling water?"

"Sparkling water it is," he said, taking two bottles from the fridge and bringing them back to the island along with ice-filled glasses.

Sitting on the bar stool adjacent to Nati's, Cade opened the bottles, poured Nati's drink and handed it to her, then poured his own, too. Then he unloaded the food from the sack, assuring her she was going to be astounded by the deliciousness of it all.

Nati could only smile at his enthusiasm as she served herself a little of everything, tasted it and agreed that it was every bit as wonderful as he thought.

Once they'd settled into eating, Nati made small talk by saying, "How was your day?"

"Crazy busy," he said. "We're opening three new stores in three states and we hit glitches with them all today."

"And you had to take care of the problems because you're… What exactly are you in the family business?"

"CEO."

"You're the head of the whole thing?" she asked, marveling at the fact that he was as young and as down to earth as he was and still held such a lofty position.

He shrugged off her astonishment as he finished a bite of puttanesca before he said, "That's my title but it isn't a big deal—"

Nati couldn't help laughing at that notion. "You're the CEO of a company that could probably rule the world and it isn't a big deal?" she said.

"Camden Incorporated is owned equally and jointly by the *family*—"

"But you are at the helm."

He shook his head. "My brothers and sister, my cousins and I form the board of directors, and we all have one vote on everything. The titles are really just formalities. Truthfully, I got mine by default."

Nati laughed. "You're the *CEO* of Camden Incorporated by *default?*"

"My older brother, Seth—who is the oldest grandchild—could have had the title because he was the first of us to graduate college and enter the workforce. But he wanted to live in Northbridge, to run the ranch there—he's cowboy through and through. What he *didn't* want was to live in Denver and wear a suit and sit behind a desk. So he opted to oversee the agricultural side of things—"

"And, since you were next up in the batting order you became CEO?"

"Yeah. But if my interests had been, say, in food—" he held a forkful of salad in the air, ate it, then continued "—I could have said all I want to deal with is the grocery end of things, and I could have done that. It just so happened that my degrees—undergrad and graduate—are in business, so I became CEO."

"That easy?" Nati asked.

"We all do whatever interests us or falls under our own special areas of expertise or education. Bottom line—what we're good at, what we enjoy doing, that's what we do."

"That seems like an unstructured way to run a major corporation," Nati observed.

"Maybe. But so far it's worked out. We're a ten-person team that gets along—maybe because no one carries more weight than anyone else. Regardless of the title, I'm still just one-tenth of the driving force behind the Camden enterprise. If I tried to pull some kind of rank or boss my siblings or cousins around, they'd just laugh, remind me that the last time I tried to do that was when I was twelve and they stranded me in the tree house, went on about their business and pretended not to know where I was until GiGi was ready to call the police."

The smile on his handsome face told her that he bore no resentments, either for that long-ago incident or for the fact that he wielded no power over his siblings and cousins in the business.

Humility was also not something Nati expected of him and she couldn't help being impressed by it.

But she reminded herself that when she'd first met her former husband, he'd also seemed like any other college boy, albeit with more money. That even after they were married, Doug had been a master at giving the right impression. And as far as she knew, what Cade was allowing her to see and what was behind the curtain could very well be two different things.

He is a Camden, after all, she told herself. His family had a reputation for doing things with subterfuge, so she shouldn't be too taken in by what she was seeing.

She decided to do a little probing.

"What exactly *do* you do as CEO?"

"Well… I guess it's like being the head of a committee. I do a lot of overseeing. And, in some ways, I'm a glorified middleman—for instance, when it comes to the agricultural part of things, Seth is in complete charge. But once he's made a decision that affects, say, supply, delivery, marketing or what-have-you, it's up to me to pass that along to the departments handling supply, delivery, marketing and what-have-you, and to deal with what happens as a result. Glorified middleman," he repeated.

Again Nati thought he was being humble, and decided to dig deeper still.

"Where did you go to college?"

His grin was pure bad boy. "I thought I should try out the beach so I did undergrad at Cal State Long Beach, and got my MBA at UCLA."

"And partied hardy?"

He laughed. "The first year. Endless rounds of fraternity and sorority parties, beach parties—you name it, there was a party attached to it. And there was the ocean and hanging out there. Pretending I was a surfer—"

"You weren't?"

"I could never stay up on those dumb boards. Mostly I laid on the sand, got a tan, drank beer and more beer and more beer, ogled girls in barely there bikinis, and generally slacked off—"

"Along with…let me guess…rich-boy-gone-wild things like professionally catered picnics that you hired limousines to take your guests to? Hot-air balloon rides to impress the girls? Taking a private plane for impromptu trips to wherever your heart desired when the urge struck? Oh, and you were near water…so what? Yachts? Racing them? Throwing gala yacht parties? And of course you rented out entire nightclubs for yourself and your friends…"

"No, none of that! I had an emergency credit card with a moderate limit, and GiGi monitored every charge on it. I may be a Camden but I didn't have access to the kind of bucks all that would take. Lazing around on the beach, drinking, partying, yeah, but what you're talking about? Maybe I should have gone to *your* college. As it was, I nearly flunked out just doing what I was doing."

"I don't believe that any school would flunk out a Camden," Nati said skeptically. She knew for a fact that, given his grades, her ex-husband would never have graduated but had remained in college semester after semester thanks to the generous donations from his father. And Doug *did* do most of the things she'd just enumerated for Cade.

"I will grant you that the hesitancy to flunk out a Camden was how I got caught," Cade admitted. "Someone from administration contacted GiGi with regrets for my poor academic performance and hinted that special concessions could be granted to me if only the college had some incentive."

"And your grandmother wrote a check?"

Cade laughed again. "GiGi was *not* going to buy anybody a degree—that's what she said. And she doesn't put up with the kind of messing around I was doing—let alone catered picnics or limos or chartered planes or yachts or hot-air balloons or any of that other stuff you were talking about. GiGi had Louie work me like a dog when I came home for summer break. She set an hourly wage, I couldn't do less than forty hours a week and she kept every penny of the money to pay back what I'd wasted in tuition."

"But she let you go back the next year?"

"She wasn't going to but I persuaded her to give me one semester to prove I'd get serious about my education. She said if I didn't she wouldn't put another penny into it and she'd see to it that the only position I ever held with Camden Inc. was doing the worst job she could muster up. And I knew she'd do it."

"Tough lady."

"Oh, yeah."

"And that straightened you up?"

"It had an impact. But like everything else, it wasn't *only* GiGi. I'd also spent a lot of years under my great-grandfather's influence, too. His goal during those years after the plane crash was to instill in all of us kids the need to carry on the family business, to build on what he'd started, and I actually did want to do that—"

"After you cut loose a little," Nati interjected.

"Sure. I was a kid," Cade admitted. "Plus I came home that summer after the first year to Margaret's disappointment in me—that was hard to take. And to some stern talks from Louie about what it means to be a decent, honorable, responsible man, one he didn't have to be embarrassed to know. That wasn't easy to hear, either—"

"So they shamed you and guilted you into shaping up?" Nati said.

"In spades," he confirmed. "From then on it was nose to the grindstone. I didn't even *join* a fraternity so I wouldn't be tempted to do too much partying. I became a studious, very dull boy."

"Who never learned to surf?"

"Never did," he said with a laugh.

They'd finished the main course. Cade pushed the take-out containers away, making room for them to share the dessert just as they had the night before. They ate from opposite ends of a stack of rum-soaked ladyfingers interlayered with cocoa-dusted Bavarian cream, both of them leaning forward as cozily as if this was something old hat to them.

"So," Cade said then, "all that catered-picnic, hot-air-balloon, private-plane stuff—what college did *you* go to?"

"The University of Colorado in Boulder. But it wasn't as if any of that stuff was officially sponsored by the college—"

His eyebrows arched high. "You mean you actually *did* all that? I thought you made it up."

"No, I actually did some of it and heard about the rest."

"The hot-air balloon?"

"I didn't do that one, no. I wasn't that brave."

"Was this connected to a sorority or something?"

"It wasn't connected to the college at all. It was just the doings of one guy. And I was…his guest," she said, settling on that definition of her relationship with Doug in college.

"One guy?" Cade repeated. "The rich boy gone wild?"

The last thing she wanted to talk about was Doug so she merely said, "No. That was—and is—just the way he lives. It was pretty amazing, though…"

"And fun, it sounds like."

"Mmm…" Nati agreed. "It's easy to get swept up in that lifestyle, that's for sure."

"How far did he sweep you?"

Nati laughed. "Far," was all she said.

Cade must have picked up on her reluctance to talk about her ex because he didn't pursue it. Instead he said, "So how were *your* grades?"

Nati laughed again, wishing he wasn't so easy to talk to, that she didn't feel as comfortable with him as she did, that she didn't enjoy every minute with him so much.

"My grades *had* to be good. I was at college on a scholarship that my grandfather's lodge awarded me."

"Full ride?"

"It had to be."

"Your family couldn't afford to pay for college...." That sobered Cade.

"I was proud of winning the scholarship and it paid for almost my whole degree. Keeping my grades up was a small price for that and I was an overachiever anyway, so I would have worked just as hard."

"You didn't have to have a kick in the pants not to be a slacker like I did?" he joked.

"Slacker," Nati echoed to tease him and lighten the tone again.

It elicited a smile from him but he still returned to the subject of her family's humble finances.

"Without the scholarship you wouldn't have been able to go to college at all?"

Nati shrugged. "It's water under the bridge, but it *was* one of the times my grandfather said it would be better if we'd been back in Northbridge—apparently there's a small college there that lets residents of the town attend for next to nothing. But the important thing is that you and I both got our degrees. And that you've come a long way, because this tiramisu is fabulous," she joked.

What remained of Cade's somberness disappeared. "All I did was bring it home, I don't think I can take any credit for the dessert itself."

Yes, she did like his humility, even when it was only in jest.

In fact, she liked everything she'd seen of Cade so

far. Which made it difficult to remember that she was supposed to be resisting his appeal.

"I'm so full I'm going to explode," she said, taking her last bite. "I have to stop." *And go home where it's safe...*

"I'll finish it," he warned.

"Go for it! This is two nights in a row of big dinners *and* dessert—are you trying to fatten me up or what?"

His gaze settled on her with a warmth and appreciation she hadn't expected. "I wouldn't change a thing, so no, I'm not trying to fatten you up. But am I spoiling myself by taking advantage of the opportunities to have your company at dinner? For that I might not have much of a defense."

And she didn't have any defense against his charm. For a moment she basked in the warmth of his eyes and his smile.

But only for a moment before she took herself to task for it and began to gather take-out containers to clean up so she could get out of there.

"I left the samples for the hope chest design on the dining room table," she said, going back to business in an attempt to steer this evening away from feeling like a date. "If your grandmother likes one of them I can get started in the next couple of days. If she doesn't I can tweak things however she wants. The light in my workshop is better than it was in the attic so I managed to make out just enough of the design around the clasp to bring back the original. I gave her a couple choices of colors. She can also decide how new or how weathered she wants it to look."

"Great. I'll get them to her and let you know. Will you be here tomorrow?"

Did he have another dinner up his sleeve? Because while one part of her would love it if he did, the smarter, saner part of her told her to avoid it.

"I will be, but I'm not sure when." That was a lie. She knew she was watching both shops in the morning and coming back to Cade's house to work in the afternoon. But she decided on the spot that she would make sure she was gone long before he might come home with more delicious food. And avoid another chance to spend time with him…

"You—or your grandmother—can call and let me know what she decides if we miss each other." Which she was going to make sure they did. "Or you can leave the sample she chooses on the table and I'll pick it up when I'm here tomorrow or the time after that, which is when I'll be done with your wall."

"Already? Seems like you just got started," he said, sounding disappointed. "Maybe I should look around and see if I need another wall done."

Instant hope sprang to life in Nati, serving to warn her even more that she was treading on dangerous ground. This was *not* a guy for her. Even if she had been ready for a new relationship, which she wasn't.

She didn't say anything more as she loaded their empty containers back into the bag. Then, glancing around the expansive silver and black state-of-the-art kitchen, she said, "Trash?"

"I'll take care of it," Cade assured, tossing the smaller container that had held the tiramisu into the bag, too. "How about after-dinner coffee or tea? Can I interest you in one of those?"

"No, thanks," she said, "I have to get going."

"I'll help you carry stuff to your car," he offered.

"I already did that." While he was showering.

Nati flushed as her traitorous mind made her imagine the man stepping out from under the spray of water, glistening wet, probably all muscular and defined and perfectly proportioned with those wide shoulders and that narrow waist.

"My jacket is still in the dining room, though," she said.

"I should probably get your samples out of there, too. If I don't put them where I'll see them when I go out I'll never remember them."

They went to the dining room together. Once they were there, it seemed strange not to lay out the drawings and samples to show to Cade.

"You do such nice work," Cade said as he looked over them. "This is exactly the original design. I like this one with the brighter, more defined colors, but I can't speak for GiGi. She may want this one that's kind of antique-looking."

"I like the brighter one, too. But I'm fine doing any of them. Or something else—make sure you let her know if she doesn't like any of these I'll go a different route."

"I will," he assured. "But GiGi isn't hard to please."

"Just let me know."

Nati's jacket was draped across the back of the chair they were both standing behind and when she reached for it Cade was quicker, grabbing it and saying, "You're sure I can't talk you into coffee or tea? Or an after-dinner brandy somebody gave me that I haven't had the chance to taste…?"

"I really have to get going," Nati said, sticking to her guns.

"Too bad," he muttered. He held her plain cotton jacket open for her as if it were a fur coat.

Nati turned her back to him and slipped her arms into the sleeves.

Then she pivoted around to face Cade again. She nodded toward the samples on the table. "Don't forget those," she advised.

Cade merely nodded without taking his eyes off her. Rather than reaching for the sample sheets, he took hold of the stand collar of her jacket and yanked it more securely around her neck.

"It's colder out there now than it was earlier today," he said, explaining the gesture.

But he didn't take his hands away once he'd adjusted the collar. He kept holding on to it. To Nati. Who tipped her head back to look up at him.

The man had the bluest, bluest eyes.

And such incredibly well-chiseled features.

And he smelled like heaven.

And the very faintest of smiles curled the corners of his mouth just before he took a little dip and kissed her.

A fragment of a split second and it was over. A mere whisper of his lips to hers—that was all it was. The same kiss of the night before, only this time it was on her mouth.

Every bit of starch went out of Nati's legs.

"Yeah. No. I probably shouldn't have done that, huh?" he said in a ragged, husky voice.

Nati shook her head. He shouldn't have kissed her but she couldn't bring herself to actually *say* it because all she really wanted was for him to do it again.

Cade took a deep breath. He drew himself up straighter before he tugged just slightly on her coat collar once more, and then released it.

"I told you that tiramisu was drenched in rum," he joked then, as if that was his excuse.

"Too good to pass up, though," Nati said quietly.

The chuckle that rumbled from Cade's throat in response made her wonder if he was thinking that it wasn't only the dessert that was too good to pass up. But it was dangerous for her to entertain the idea that he thought she was, too.

When he went on standing there, looking at her, making her wonder if he was considering kissing her again despite knowing that he shouldn't, Nati scooped up the sample pages and handed them to him.

"Don't forget these," she said.

He accepted them from her and that was when Nati decided she should make her escape.

She turned and led the way out of the dining room to the front door where Cade set the sample pages on a table in his entry and maneuvered himself into a position to open the door for her.

"Thanks for dinner—again."

"Thanks for having it with me," he countered.

Nati went out onto the front landing, glad to be in the chill of the evening air suddenly and hoping it would shock her to her senses since all she could think about was kissing Cade again.

Especially when he stepped outside with her onto

the small stoop that didn't provide for much distance between them.

He leaned a shoulder against the doorjamb, which put him more on her eye level.

"If I don't see you before I finish with your wall, I'll just send you the final bill and you can mail me a check," she said then.

"Or you can hold off until you finish with the hope chest, too, and I'll come pick it up and settle everything at once."

"Sure, that would work. I can send the bill, though, in case you get busy or something and would rather that I deliver the hope chest to your grandmother."

"Okay," Cade said, a frown tugging at his forehead as if he didn't like the possibility that they might not be seeing each other again.

But it would be for the best if they didn't, Nati thought.

Or at least that was what the rational part of her thought.

Then there was that other, not-so-rational part that was still thinking about the kiss that had happened just moments before. It had been so fleeting. And she wanted to repeat it right there and then....

She leaned forward, tempted. Oh so tempted to kiss him this time. Longer and harder and deeper...

And was he leaning slightly in her direction, too?

It would have been so easy to kiss him. To have just one more that she could register in her memory.

But she took a really deep breath, forced herself to step back, and said, "I'm just gonna go now...."

Cade didn't encourage or discourage her. He merely

watched as she left the stoop and headed for her car in the driveway.

She didn't glance in the direction of the front door again until she'd slipped behind the steering wheel.

And even though she was hoping that Cade might have gone back inside by then, he hadn't. He was still standing outside, one broad shoulder against the jamb, his hands in his rear jean pockets, watching her.

As she started her engine and put her car into reverse Cade took one hand out and waved. All Nati did to acknowledge the gesture was raise her chin before she backed out of his drive, knowing she had to get out of there. That she had to get home to the small, no-frills house in Arden where she'd grown up.

And away from the man who was more temptation than she had the strength to resist.

Chapter Six

"I have time for one fast cup of coffee, and then I need to get to work," Cade told his grandmother when he showed up at her house early the next morning. "I just wanted to bring you these samples Nati Morrison left for the design on the hope chest. As soon as she knows how you want it, she'll get started."

GiGi poured him the coffee, and then sat with him in the breakfast nook with her own half-finished cup. "How are things going with her?"

Last night's kiss flashed through Cade's mind the minute his grandmother asked that. Not even a sleepless night of telling himself that he'd taken a very wrong turn prevented him from wanting to kiss her again. And better the next time...

"She's great," he heard himself say. "Not that it matters, but she seems like a nice person."

GiGi stared at him over her coffee cup, then took a

sip without saying anything. She seemed a little suspicious.

"When it comes to our real project with the Morrisons I've just barely skimmed the surface. I can't really say yet whether or not what H.J. did back in Northbridge caused long-term damage. Or even if there's resentment about it. Things changed for the Morrisons when they lost that farm, but so far I'm not sure their lives would have been remarkably better or worse if they'd stayed in Northbridge. Everything we've talked about so far has been kind of superficial."

"So you'll keep trying," GiGi said.

"Yeah. I'm just not exactly sure how to 'keep trying' without it seeming like dating." Which was what every minute with Nati so far had felt like. Very, very good dates. Dates he didn't want to end. Dates that left him itching to see her again.

"You don't want to mislead her," GiGi said, reading his thoughts, as if she knew that there were things simmering inside of him when it came to Nati.

"No, I don't want to mislead her. Of course not. That's the problem."

"And you can't just talk with her, get to know about her and her family in a friendly way?"

Sure, he *should* be able to do that. It just wasn't working out that way. Probably because being with Nati just didn't feel like chatting with a stranger. He wasn't exactly sure why that was, now that he thought about it. It just was. She was easy to be with, they had similar senses of humor, she was smart and quick-witted and interesting, she was warm and open. When he was with her there was just some kind of connection that seemed to override everything else—including his own good sense and better judgment.

So much so that he kept losing sight of the fact that she could be harboring some deeply rooted animosity toward all Camdens. Animosity that she could take out on him in some way down the road. So much so that he kept letting down his guard and forgetting that she could start to see dollar signs every time she looked at him and that that could land him in the kind of mess he'd found himself in twice before.

"The problem is," he said after a moment of reflection, "she's going to finish with my wall and when she does there isn't a reason to see her at all."

"Have her do another wall."

"I thought of that. Maybe. I don't know. I'll figure something out," he said. "For now, when you decide what you want her to do with the hope chest I can relay that information and that'll give me another excuse to see her."

GiGi glanced at the samples and pointed to the one that looked more aged. "This," she decreed.

"Okay. I'll tell her."

Cade finished his coffee and took his cup to the sink to rinse it and put it in the dishwasher, thinking as he did that the situation with Nati was just more complicated than he could convey to his grandmother.

Nati was off-limits and that was all there was to it, but he was having so damn much trouble keeping that in mind when he was with her.

Because as soon as he was, it started to seem like things could work out between them. And all of his resolve, all of his determination, all of his memories of courts and lawyers and false accusations and ugliness, all of his reasons to keep his distance, just flew out the window.

But he had to quit letting that happen.

Think paternity claim, he told himself. *Think breach of promise...*

Because those were both situations he never—ever—wanted to get sucked into again. So he couldn't take any risks.

Which meant that no matter how good it felt to be with Nati, it couldn't go anywhere.

Not anywhere beyond this errand his grandmother had sent him on.

And certainly not anywhere near where he kept wanting it to go.

"Oh, no," Nati muttered to herself.

She'd had such determination today. Such resolve.

She'd fully intended to do the work she needed to do on Cade's wall that Wednesday afternoon and get out of there long before there was any chance whatsoever of him coming home. Of her seeing him. Of getting drawn in by him. Of ending up kissing him again.

She was also determined to make sure she didn't see him on Friday, either—when she would complete her work in his house. Then she'd send him a bill and do everything she could to never set eyes on the man again.

But her stupid, stupid car had conked out. With plenty of time to spare, she'd left Cade's house, slipped behind the wheel, put the key in the ignition and turned it. And nothing had happened. No matter what she did.

So at four-fifteen she'd had to call a tow truck. That

was almost three hours ago and when the tow truck had finally pulled up and she'd learned that she wasn't allowed to catch a ride back to Arden in the truck, she'd called a cab. But just when the tow truck driver was locking in the chains that kept her car secure, just when the cab arrived, so did Cade.

Looking as terrific as always in tweed dress pants and a black mock turtleneck sweater.

"What's going on?" he asked as he approached her where she stood on the curb. He'd been forced to park there since he couldn't get near his driveway due to the tow truck.

"My car wouldn't start," Nati said.

"And the cab?"

"To take me back to my shop. I need to get my scarecrow over to the festival organizer by eight. I thought I could just ride with the tow truck driver but he says that for insurance reasons the company can take my car but not me. I couldn't get hold of my grandfather—he hasn't been home and he's not good about keeping his cell phone turned on or even remembering to take it with him half the time. Holly couldn't come—someone left her three dogs to groom today and still hasn't picked them up, and since I don't know anything about where to catch a bus or which bus would get me back to Arden, I was out of other options."

And if only he'd been ten minutes later. Then she wouldn't be standing here adoring the sight of him with a little stubble that only added to his appeal.

"I'm not going to let you pay for a cab," Cade decreed, heading in the direction of the waiting taxi.

"No, it's fine, really... Please..." Nati called after

him, unable to pursue him because just then the tow truck driver was coming her way with a clipboard.

Cade didn't acknowledge her plea. When he reached the cabby's window, he leaned over to the talk to him. The view of Cade's great rear end gave Nati a hot flash, and she scolded herself for that, saying, "Really, this is not your problem. Please just tell him I'll be there in a minute…."

But still Cade ignored her.

She saw him pass something through the window and hoped that he was merely paying the cabby in advance. But she had those hopes dashed when the cab drove away.

Nati signed what the tow truck driver wanted her to sign and gave him the address of her mechanic. He returned to his truck about the time that Cade rejoined her and said, "I'll get you wherever you need to go."

"I'm working for you," she said as if they both needed to be reminded of that. "You don't take any of your other employees home, do you?"

"If they need a ride I do," he said.

The loud rumble of the tow truck's engine was too much to talk over. When it drove off, Nati was once again alone with Cade.

And fighting an unreasonable sense of delight that she knew she shouldn't be feeling.

"Let me call another cab," she said, because being with him poked a hole in her willpower and she already knew where that could land her.

"No chance. Come on, let's get you to your shop, and then I'll help you with that freaky scarecrow, too."

And that's how it starts, Nati thought, doubting that

he would accept her rejection of his offer to help with the scarecrow any more than he'd accepted her rejection of his offer to drive her back to the suburbs.

"Don't you need to go inside first?" she asked.

"No, I'm good. I even ate—I had a dinner meeting with my brother and sister. But what about you? I'll bet you haven't had anything since lunch—"

"Actually, when the tow company said it would be a two-hour wait—which ended up being a *three*-hour wait—I walked over to Cherry Creek Mall and grabbed a slice of pizza. I just need to get back to my shop."

"Then let's go," Cade suggested, moving to the passenger side of his car to open the door for her.

With a sigh of resignation, Nati got in and he closed the door behind her.

The car smelled of his cologne. While he walked around to get in the driver's side Nati closed her eyes and took a deep breath, breathing it in as if it were life's oxygen before she realized what she was doing and forced her eyes open.

What was wrong with her?

She really was acting like a crazy, infatuated kid.

Vowing to stop, she sat up straight and stiff and put on her seat belt just as Cade slipped behind the steering wheel.

As they drove, Nati stuck strictly to business, reporting on the status of his wall, telling him that she would be finished sanding and polishing it by Friday.

Just as they were getting on the highway Cade's cell phone rang. He checked the display and said it was a call he had to take. His side of a business conversation filled the rest of the drive to Arden, ending only when they pulled into the small parking lot behind her shop.

"I'm sorry about that," he said as he put his phone away.

"It's okay. Business. I understand," Nati said, more concerned over the fact that her grandfather's car was parked in the lot, too. And that he was just crossing the street from his lodge at that moment.

When it was originally built, Old Town had only needed to accommodate horses and buggies, so the streets were narrow. Parking areas were at a minimum. One of the few parking lots in the neighborhood was behind the building that housed Nati and Holly's shops. Whenever Jonah went to the lodge and couldn't get a spot in its tiny lot, he parked in Nati's.

And now here he came. And here was Cade Camden.

"You can just drop me off," Nati said, hoping that might actually work.

But of course it didn't. "I don't have anything to do tonight. I'll help you get your scarecrow and take it wherever it needs to go and maybe we can check out that ice-cream shop over there." He nodded in the direction of the newly opened ice-cream parlor that promised old-fashioned, dreamy, creamy ice cream.

About that time Nati's grandfather spotted her in Cade's passenger seat and waved. Then Cade parked in the spot next to Jonah's car.

"My grandfather," Nati said by way of explanation as she waved back, getting out of the car as soon as Cade had come to a stop.

"I've been trying to call you," Nati said to her grandfather. "My car died and had to be towed."

"Oh… I'm sorry. I left my phone at home," Jonah said contritely. "I was playing poker."

Cade got out and came around to join them. There was nothing Nati could do but introduce them, so that's what she did.

Cade extended a hand for her grandfather to shake, and they exchanged amenities before Jonah said, "So you're Georgianna's grandson. How is she?"

"She's doing well. I know she'd want me to send her regards. She speaks highly of you."

"She was always a good gal. The best thing about old Northbridge. Does she still make those oatmeal raisin cookies?"

Cade laughed and assured Jonah that she did, and while the two of them rhapsodized about the cookies, Nati relaxed.

She didn't know what she'd expected to happen if they came face-to-face, but the thought of it had made her instantly tense. Not only was there a less-than-desirable history between the Morrisons and the Camdens, but she'd had flashbacks to the way Doug had always behaved around her family—patronizing, condescending, disdainful—and she'd feared the same would be true of Cade.

Instead Cade was faultlessly respectful, congenial and friendly, and her grandfather was his usual warm, open self.

"Well, tell Georgianna that I said hello," Jonah said after announcing that he needed to get going to meet a friend by eight.

Cade promised that he would.

Turning to Nati, Jonah offered to pick her up later.

But Nati rejected that idea. She told her grandfather that she'd get home in the old truck that was now parked alongside the building. She used it only as needed to make occasional deliveries for the shop, but it still ran, so her grandfather accepted that solution, agreed that they'd talk in the morning and left.

"I have to get that scarecrow to Gus before he goes home," Nati said a bit frantically, digging in her purse for her keys to let them in the store's rear door.

She was grateful for Cade's help after all. The scarecrow was no small thing to maneuver but he managed to do it easily and they got to the sandwich shop just as Gus Spurgis was turning the sign hanging on the inside of his door from open to closed.

Gus took the scarecrow, and told her he'd be putting them all up at various spots around Old Town the next day before making it clear that he wanted to get home.

Then Nati found herself back out on the sidewalk with Cade, who leaned close to her ear and whispered, "Ice cream!"

She couldn't help laughing as she realized that all of her good intentions today were floating away in October's evening breeze and she was just happy to be with him.

"Ice cream," she conceded. "But only if you let me buy—it's the least I can do for saving me cab fare."

"Deal."

Ten minutes later they were sitting at a café table enjoying their ice cream and paying no attention to the flier the shop owner had given Cade inviting them to the wine and cheese tasting that was being held the next night to launch the Scarecrow Festival.

"This is great!" Cade decreed of his mint chocolate chip.

"Mine, too," Nati said, almost missing a drop of triple chocolate that threatened to fall from her spoon down the front of the tan-colored turtleneck sweater.

"It was nice to meet your grandfather."

"Thanks for being friendly to him."

Cade frowned in confusion. "Why wouldn't I be friendly to him?"

She'd spoken out of her own past experience with Doug and her in-laws, and wasn't too sure how to explain what she meant without getting into that topic.

So she hedged. "Oh, you know how it is. Some people aren't comfortable meeting family and they can come off…I don't know, *un*friendly, I guess. Cold. As if they think they're better…"

"Yeah, I've met a few people like that. I didn't like them. I definitely don't want to be one of them."

He paused for a moment as if he were judging his next words before he said, "Just between you and me, my grandmother feels bad about the history between her and your grandfather."

"My grandfather feels bad about that, too," Nati said. It had felt awkward to be introducing the grandson of the woman who had been rejected, to the man who had rejected her.

"He said he was just too young and he still had too many wild oats to sow," Nati went on. "He just wasn't ready to settle down. But he only has glowing things to say about your grandmother—I can tell he genuinely cared about her. They were just too young."

Cade really looked confused now. His brow was

creased over those penetrating blue eyes. "Am I hearing that right? I know your grandfather and my grandmother were high school sweethearts, but are you saying that your grandfather dumped my grandmother?"

"You didn't know that?"

"No. When GiGi has talked about him being her first love and the fact that they broke up just before she met my grandfather, she never says that it was your grandfather who did the breaking up."

Nati wondered if she'd revealed something she shouldn't have. "Your grandmother wanted to get married right out of high school—"

"Which she basically did. She married my grandfather the February after she'd graduated."

"But she and my grandfather broke up *at* graduation because he wasn't ready to get as serious as she wanted them to."

Cade chuckled at that, and it was a relief to Nati, who was beginning to think she might have opened a can of worms. "I'll be damned. All these years and that little devil left that out. She's only said it was good that they broke up because it left her free when she met my grandfather."

"Don't tell her I told you," Nati beseeched him. "Nobody wants to be reminded of being dumped." Then something else occurred to her and she said, "So if that wasn't what your grandmother feels bad about..."

It dawned on Nati belatedly what he'd been referring to. "Oh, the farm..."

With a chagrined sort of lift to his eyebrows, Cade said, "I didn't know whether to talk about it or not, but I keep feeling like it's the elephant in the room. Maybe we should. GiGi only recently found out how that went down and she *does* feel bad about it."

"She only recently found out about it? Surely she knew that my great-grandparents had the farm foreclosed on, that that was why they left Northbridge."

"She did. But she thought it was the bank that did the foreclosing. She thought that H.J. just bought the farm from the bank after the fact. All these years that's what she's believed and then some things came to light and she learned that it was H.J. who took over the mortgage from the bank and orchestrated the foreclosure. He was worried that she might still have feelings for your grandfather and..." Cade shrugged apologetically. "H.J. was not one to sit back and just let things run their course. He thought your grandfather was a threat to my grandfather getting the girl he wanted. If GiGi had known what was really going on back then she would have never stood for it. And she *hates* that that's what was done to your family. Especially over her."

"I can't deny that my great-grandparents were hurt by it," Nati admitted. "They'd had a few bad crop years and were behind in their mortgage payments. Usually the bank was understanding and gave some leeway until things had a chance to turn around for the farmers in the area. It came as a surprise to find out that their mortgage had been bought out from under them and that they were being foreclosed on."

"So it was really rough on your great-grandparents," Cade said with sympathy and regret.

"It was," Nati admitted. "Of course when I knew them I was just a little kid and they were pretty old. But even then I can remember them ranting and raving if the name Camden was in the news. And from what my grandfather has said, yes, they did have it rough after losing the farm. They basically came to Denver with nothing. My great-grandfather was hired as someone's gardener for a little while, but then he had a stroke—"

"From the stress?" Cade asked, clearly bearing the weight of what she was telling him.

"That's always been the theory," Nati confirmed. "After the stroke he couldn't work, and my great-grandmother needed to take care of him, so neither could she. That left it all up to my grandfather—he supported his parents from then until they died."

"Wow. I'm kind of surprised *he* was friendly to *me* just now...."

Nati laughed. "That's just the person he is. He actually never thought your grandmother knew about what H. J. Camden did. He's always given her the benefit of the doubt. He'll probably be glad to know he was right. But he's a really positive, upbeat person—he's the king of making lemonade out of lemons."

"So would you say that he's basically been happy with the way his life turned out?"

Nati could see that Cade was looking for reassurance, possibly for his grandmother as well as for himself. "Yes. He always says that he plays whatever cards life deals him. When it comes to your great-grandfather and the farm, it isn't as if he's thankful that that happened. And I know he has some guilt for the fact that his involvement with your grandmother was to blame for what his parents suffered. But he made the best of it and put it behind him. I also know that he doesn't like thinking that he might have hurt your grandmother in any way."

Cade smiled wryly. "He's worried that she was hurt, she's worried that he was. That sounds like two people who still might care about each other, doesn't it?"

"Well, you know, first love..."

They finished their ice cream as the shop was closing, so they threw away their napkins, spoons and the plastic bowls, and left.

As they walked back to Nati's store Cade glanced at the flier the ice cream shop owner had given him.

"So what's this?" he asked.

"A wine and cheese tasting—the wine shop and the cheese shop joined forces to put on the first event of the Scarecrow Festival," Nati explained. "There's a big effort being made to draw people back into Old Town. Events—especially seasonal events like the Scarecrow Festival—are part of that and we're all doing anything we can because what brings more people here means more business for everyone."

"Then the wine and cheese tasting benefits you and your shop in the long run—that sounds like something that should be supported. I'm free tomorrow night. What do you say we go? Or did you already have plans for it?"

She didn't. Holly couldn't make it and Nati didn't want to go alone.

But to go with Cade?

She could rationalize the meals she'd shared with him so far. They were unplanned. But going together to the wine and cheese tasting tomorrow night? How could she not look at that as *not* a date even if he did couch it in terms of the fact that it would benefit her business?

So she knew she should refuse.

But *should* and *could?* Two different things when the temptation was intense to have a *real* date with Cade, to spend the entire evening with him without pretense, to do something she wanted to do anyway.

"I didn't have plans to go," she said, managing a little restraint.

"But it sounds like fun. What could be bad about wine and cheese? And it's for a good cause—to boost your business."

True enough.

But she still *shouldn't...*

Except that just as they reached the front of her building temptation overtook her and she heard herself say, "Okay."

"Great! It says here that it starts at eight, so I'll pick you up at seven-thirty?"

"Seven-forty-five would be fine. I only live a little ways from here."

Taking out his smartphone, Cade had her give him her address.

"It's my grandfather's house," she explained. "I live in the basement and come and go from around back, so if you just call when you get there—"

"Will massive guard dogs attack if I go around to your door to pick you up?"

"No, there aren't any dogs, it's just easier—"

"I'll come around and get you," he said in a tone that broached no further argument.

Nati pointed to an alley between the building that

housed her shop and an old house being used as a real estate office. "The truck is over there," she said. "I should start it and let it run for a few minutes—I haven't driven it in a couple of weeks. But you don't need to wait."

Cade craned to see what she was talking about. "Looks dark over there. I'll keep you company," he said.

By then Nati knew it was a waste of breath to try to keep him from doing the gentlemanly thing, so she didn't bother. She merely led him around the front of her and Holly's shops to the dark side of the building.

Unlocking the old truck and opening the door produced a dim glow from the dome light that helped illuminate the alleyway. She got in and started the engine. As it sputtered to life, the light dimmed momentarily and then brightened again.

Cade had come to stand in the open door so she pivoted on the seat to face him. She was at a height that put her eye-to-eye with the tall man.

"I won't tell my grandmother this, but I have to say that I'm kind of glad your grandfather didn't marry her," he said, a small smile making creases at the corners of his eyes. "If she had, you and I could have ended up brother and sister. Or at least cousins."

"Would that have been so bad?" Nati asked.

"Given what's on my mind right now? Really, really bad," he confided in a voice that was deeper than usual.

Nati couldn't help smiling at that revelation. There was an undeniable energy charging the air all of a sudden. And she knew what was going to happen. Cade was going to kiss her. And she also knew that she *should* stop it.

But her chin tipped up ever so slightly instead, and she looked into his eyes the way he was looking into hers—intently, longingly.

"Ahh...what is it that you do to me, Morrison..." he whispered, in the throes of his own overwhelming temptation.

Then he slid one arm along the top of the truck's seat back, grabbed the steering wheel with his other hand, and leaned forward gradually to take her mouth with his.

Nati's eyes drifted closed and she accepted the kiss, returned it, her mind chasing away all thoughts.

Slow and steady and thoughtful, this was not like the kisses that had come before. This was not impulsive or stolen. This was a kiss that got to be a kiss in all its glory.

With their breaths mingling and their lips easing into it, Nati savored the full feel of just how agile and talented a kisser Cade was. The kiss was sweet and soft, then firmer, deeper. Their heads swayed the tiniest bit, mouths fitted together like two halves making a whole, and it went on long enough for every nuance to imprint on Nati's memory.

She didn't want it to end when it did. But after a moment, Cade brought it to a conclusion, pushed himself out of the truck cab and stood up straight.

Tonight he made no apologies or excuses. Instead he stayed looking into her eyes for a long moment.

Nati thought he was going to kiss her again—she *wanted* him to kiss her again.

But he didn't. He just went on looking at her, studying her as if he wasn't quite sure what to make of her before he said, "Tomorrow night. Seven-forty-five. Wine and cheese."

Nati nodded, not wanting to speak, not wanting to move her lips and lose the sensation of his kiss.

He reached an arm under her knees, swiveled her to face the steering wheel, locked the door and closed it.

Nati watched him in the side mirror as he walked away toward the back of the building where his own car was parked.

The scent of his cologne lingered in the truck's cab and the feel of his mouth lingered on hers from the kiss.

She had no doubt she would relive that kiss again and again in bed tonight as images of Cade played behind her closed eyelids. They would keep her from sleeping the same way they had every night since she'd first set eyes on him.

Because despite knowing better, she was having no luck at all fighting this feeling.

Fighting him.

Fighting what she knew could ultimately be very, very bad for her.

Chapter Seven

"Hit me, Holly. Hit me hard enough to knock the stupid out of me," Nati ordered as she stood in front of the full-length mirror in her bedroom, inspecting herself one last time after getting ready for her date with Cade.

She was wearing winter-white wool slacks and a matching cashmere cowl-neck sweater. Her hair framed her face in a perfect, shiny fall. A hint of makeup accentuated her cheekbones, mascara lengthened her eyelashes, and a pale lipstick made her lips a glossy pink. She'd even given her short nails a fresh manicure.

Holly, who had come to borrow a pair of earrings for her own blind date, took in the finished product. "You may have gotten the short end of the stick in that marriage to Doug, but you did come out of it with some nice clothes."

"And those earrings—they're the only piece of jewelry I didn't sell to bankroll the shop."

Holly held them out to her. "Maybe you should wear them tonight."

"They're too fancy for this outfit. Plus, this wine and cheese tasting in Old Town is more casual than that. Just don't lose them—at three carats apiece they're my rainy-day fund."

"I'll guard them with my life. But I won't hit you," Holly said, returning to Nati's earlier demand.

"What am I doing?" Nati asked in response. "I've only been divorced six months. And the first guy I *do* go out with isn't Mr. Every Man, he's another rich boy! Richer than the last one!"

"Maybe it isn't the rich-boy thing that you should be thinking about. Maybe you should just be thinking about how he's your first guy after the divorce."

Nati laughed. "That sounds like you mean he's the first of many."

"I do. Even if he's not the first of *many,* he's the first. The back-in-the-saddle-again guy. The get-your-feet-wet-again guy. The guy who lets you know that you can get out there again and mingle and meet other guys until you find the right one."

"The first guy, not the keeper?"

"Exactly. The practice guy just to get you back in the game."

"'Back in the saddle,' 'get your feet wet,' 'get back out there,' 'get back in the game'—there are a lot of sayings for that."

"Because there are so many of us who find ourselves in that position. And now you're one of us. But you keep talking about this guy as if he's the one. He's only dangerous if you get in as deep with him as you did with

Doug. Deep enough for prenups, and marriage, and family and social pressures, and relationship and maturity and…other…problems, and then divorce, and the whole mess. But Cade Camden isn't all that. He's just a guy you can get some refresher-dating practice with."

"That's true," Nati agreed, seeing her friend's point of view. "I do keep jumping the gun, don't I?"

"It's like there's a fire five hundred miles away and you've been burned," Holly reasoned. "Of course your instinct is to run in the other direction. But the fire is way—*way*—in the distance—"

"So maybe I'm making too big a deal out of this."

"I say be careful. But yeah, maybe a little spark for this guy is a good sign—it tells us you're rising from the ashes."

"But it doesn't have to be any more than that," Nati concluded.

"It doesn't."

But what if it was?

That question nagged at Nati. She'd never had the same reaction to anyone that she was having to Cade. Not even with Doug. She couldn't stop thinking about Cade every minute of every day. And never had she wanted to be with anyone—wanted anyone—like she wanted that man.

But maybe that was only because she was raw. She was so fresh from her marriage, her divorce, maybe her emotions were just closer to the surface than they usually were, causing the intensity of her attraction to Cade.

Maybe if she relaxed a little, she'd get some perspective and see that Cade really was just the initial stepping stone to get her back in the game—as Holly had said.

And if that was the case, then it was actually healthy for her to give in a little to what was happening with Cade.

"I have to get going," Holly said, interrupting Nati's reflections. "Don't beat yourself up anymore—or ask anyone else to beat you up, either—over this thing tonight. It isn't stupid, it's just spending some time with a guy—good for the ego. And yours could use a boost."

"That seems a little mercenary—I'm just going out with him to boost my own ego?"

"He gets the pleasure of your company, that's his reward," Holly said loftily, making Nati laugh.

"Lucky, lucky man," Nati said facetiously.

"Yes, he is," Holly insisted. "And don't you forget it—no matter who he is or how much he's worth, he's lucky to be with you."

"No matter what the Pirfoys might think?"

"History! Ancient history. We've moved on and tonight is just part of that," Holly assured her.

And as her friend left, Nati told herself that that's exactly how she was going to view tonight—as the first step toward moving on.

And nothing else.

Even if her pulse did race at the thought that Cade could be there anytime now and she knew that the minute she saw him she'd be putty in his hands.

Because that's the way it had been since they'd met.

"Wow, don't you look amazing." Cade's appreciative gaze traveled up and down her body when Nati opened the apartment door to his knock at precisely seven forty-five Thursday evening.

"Thank you. You don't clean up bad yourself," she countered.

As usual, he looked wonderful. He was wearing a pair of gray wool slacks and a black mock turtleneck sweater under a tweed sport coat that accentuated the breadth of his shoulders. He stood tall and straight and commanding, and Nati just wanted to stay there and ogle him.

But instead she snatched up her own calf-length wool coat and slipped it on in a hurry, saying as she did, "Shall we go?" rather than asking him inside. She was a little afraid that if she did, she wouldn't want to go out again at all.

Cade took a step back to let her out. She pulled the door closed behind them and led the way around to the front of her grandfather's redbrick house where Cade's car was parked on the street.

"Any news on your car?" he asked, eyeing the old shop truck under her carport.

"It needs a new alternator and there's a hole in the radiator. It's basically aged-out. But I can't afford to replace it, so the mechanic will do what he can to resuscitate it again—he's good that way. It'll take him until next week."

"So maybe your bonus for a job well done needs to be new wheels?"

He had to be joking….

"I don't think so," Nati said firmly just in case he wasn't.

"I do know a couple of car dealers—why don't you at least let me talk to them, see if I can't get you a deal," he suggested as he held the passenger door open for her and she got in.

"Thanks, but no—"

He closed the door, went around the rear of the car and got in. "I'm sure I could get you a demo car or something for dirt cheap and—"

"No, really," Nati insisted. "When mine absolutely can't be fixed anymore I'll work it out." Probably by selling the earrings that Holly was wearing tonight unless business improved enough to allow for a car payment. But she wasn't going to go into her financial situation with Cade.

"I'd like to help," Cade said with a sideways glance at her just before he pulled away from the curb.

"And I like being able to do things without help." Because the last time she'd needed and accepted it, it had cost her dearly. "But thanks for the offer."

"It's open-ended—if you change your mind. You need a reliable car to get wherever your work takes you, you know…."

"I do know. And mine will be fine. It has a few more years in it."

"But you'll keep me in mind—"

"Sure," she said without camouflaging the fact that there was no chance she would ever factor him into it.

She was glad when they reached Old Town just then so they could stop talking about it.

"Park behind my shop and we can walk," she instructed, wondering why Cade had that troubled frown on his face that she'd seen in the past.

He pulled into her lot without saying more about her car predicament. The wine and cheese tasting event had apparently drawn a crowd because all four of the spots in her lot were already being used. Cade ended up parking in the dark, narrow area between her building and the real estate office.

Still, though, it was nice to see a good turn-out and Nati hoped that whoever had used her parking lot would do some window shopping and come back to the store to buy something or hire her for in-home work.

The wine and cheese tasting was crowded. It was organized in stations where particular wines were paired with their complementary cheeses. Someone from either the cheese or wine shop was standing at every station to point out why the pairings worked.

The setup wasn't conducive to a lot of conversation, but it was still fun, and by the time Nati and Cade had visited all of the stations, Nati had had enough sips of wine to help her mellow out.

Before they left, Cade bought a case of Chianti Classico and an entire wheel of the Pecorino Toscana cheese that had been served drizzled with garlic-infused olive oil and sprinkled with grains of sea salt. Nati carried the wheel of cheese while Cade carried the wine back to his car.

"You must have *really* liked these," Nati observed as he opened the narrow trunk.

"We came to support your fellow local businesses, didn't we?"

"Sure," Nati allowed. "But buying one or two bottles of wine and a little cheese would have accomplished that."

"They were great, though. And this isn't all for me. I'll keep one bottle of the wine and a wedge of the cheese, and give the same to GiGi, to Margaret and Louie, and to each of my siblings and cousins—that'll take care of all twelve bottles and the whole wheel."

"That's very thoughtful of you," Nati observed as they got into his car and headed back to her place.

Cade shrugged off the compliment. "We all do it. If we find something we like, we share. It's always been that way. Except maybe for Seth—he probably gets the short end here and there because he's in Northbridge. I'll send him the wine but he'll miss out on the cheese."

Cade grinned, then added, "Not that he'll care this round. He just got engaged and he's so into his fiancée Lacey that I don't think he notices anything else."

"Seth is your older brother, right? The one who abdicated as CEO?"

"Right."

"And he's getting married?"

"To Lacey Kincaid—she's the daughter of Morgan Kincaid—"

"The big football guy who owns a bunch of restaurants and things? There's one of his restaurants in Cherry Creek, isn't there? Kincaid's?"

"Right. He also just brought an NFL football franchise to Montana and he's building a training center in Northbridge. Lacey is heading up that project—that's how she and Seth met. She also has an internet business selling women's sports clothes. Seth says she's learning to delegate and not be so work obsessed. Anyway… I don't know how I got off on that tangent. But Seth will get wine and no cheese."

They'd arrived back at Nati's house. Cade parked at

the curb and reached into the side pocket on his door, pulling out a tall, thin bottle.

"The framboise you liked so well—I thought I'd surprise you. Now you can have more than a sip."

Nati *had* loved that dessert wine and coveted a bottle but she hadn't thought it showed.

"You didn't have to do that," she said in spite of the fact that she was glad he had.

"Didn't *have* to, *wanted* to," he said, getting out of the car and coming around to Nati's side just as she got out, too.

She'd been weighing whether or not to invite him in before that. She'd enjoyed the wine and cheese tasting but it hadn't been an occasion that had left her feeling like she'd really spent the time with Cade. Then on top of that the evening had ended too quickly. Now, as Cade walked her to her door she had reason to say, "Maybe you should come in and we should open the framboise…."

He grinned at her as he held the gate so she could go into the backyard ahead of him. "I think that's a fine idea."

"I have to warn you, though, it isn't an impressive place. And I only own water and juice glasses…."

"Oh, no, not juice glasses!" he joked, clearly unfazed by her lesser accommodations.

Nati hoped that wasn't merely an act.

She unlocked her door. It opened into her kitchen and she flipped on the lights as she went in.

"This is the kitchen," she said needlessly. "That's the living room on the other side of the bar. There's a bathroom through there, too, and one bedroom—not impressive but—"

"Cozy," Cade finished for her. "And it all looks new even though the house isn't. Did you say this is your grandfather's place? But not your grand*mother's*..."

"We lost her three years ago," Nati said sadly.

"But is this the same house where you grew up?"

"It is. The reason this all looks new is that until a few months ago it was just an open basement. But I needed a place and my grandfather needed some help with expenses, so I designed this, hired a contractor and voilà!" Paid for by selling her engagement and wedding rings.

"So your grandfather lives upstairs?"

"He does," Nati confirmed while taking off her coat. She went the short distance into the living room to toss it across an antique upholstered bench.

Cade took off his sport coat and followed her lead, laying it atop hers before they both went back to the kitchen.

Nati found a corkscrew and gave Cade wine-opening duty while she retrieved two of the juice glasses she'd warned him about from the cupboard. He removed the cork and poured them each a glass of the raspberry liqueur, and Nati led the way back to the living room.

There was only one choice of seating because Nati hadn't been able to afford much furniture. In addition to the antique bench, there was a sofa, coffee and end table, floor lamp, table lamp and a small entertainment center. As Nati turned on the lamps, Cade sat on the couch—not quite at one end, not quite in the middle.

When Nati joined him she told herself to hug the

other arm of the sofa to keep as much distance as she could from him.

But since they were both sitting at an angle, her knees came very near to touching his.

Trying not to think about that, Nati made small talk about his family. "You and your brothers and sister and cousins—you grew up together, you work together—you're really close…."

"We're a tight-knit group. Hurt one, make enemies of us all."

"That's kind of a scary thought," Nati said, thinking that it had been bad enough to have the Pirfoys united against her—mother, father and Doug. The prospect of having ten *Camdens* and their grandmother as enemies—and probably Margaret and Louie in the mix—was far, far more daunting.

"Except that we're not such a scary lot," Cade demurred. "We're just close. Family comes first and always has. If one of us hits a rough patch, the rest of us are there. And when one of us brings someone in—like Lacey—she becomes part of the family, too, and we'll all be there for her just the same."

Unless the marriage doesn't work out, and then you'll all be out to get her....

Still daunting.

But even these thoughts didn't stop Nati from noticing the way the not-bright lamplight cast shadows in the hollows of his chiseled face and how rugged and sexy that made him look.

"Wasn't there *ever* dissension in the ranks? Even when you were kids or rebellious teenagers?" she asked.

He laughed. "Sure there were disagreements and

fights and arguments growing up. That was actually when H.J. instigated the one-kid, one-vote system. Sometimes disagreements went to committee and we all had a say in who we supported and who we thought was wrong. Or, with the girls, there were silent treatments or freeze-outs, and then they'd make up. With the boys sometimes there were knock-down-drag-out fights—then we'd have to take it outside and more often than not it ended with Louie turning the hose on us. But basically it taught us all how to work together. And no matter how mad we might have ever been at one another, we were still a united front outside of the family if someone else had a problem with one of us."

"And with ten of you that was a big united front..." Nati observed. "You didn't really even need outside friends, did you?"

"Sure we did," Cade said. "We're all still individuals, with different interests and personalities. And no matter how much you like your family, you need other people in your life. You need outlets. And something for yourself alone," he said in a way that seemed aimed pointedly at her and managed to give her a tiny rush.

Stopping herself from looking into those blue eyes of his, Nati finished her framboise and set the glass on the coffee table.

When she sat back she said, "I always wanted a brother or a sister. Holly was as close as I ever came, but she had two sisters of her own and there were—and still are—times when I just couldn't be a part of it. No matter how close Holly and I were, Christmas morning it was still just me and the adults."

"That's kind of sad," Cade said sympathetically.

"No, not really *sad*—it wasn't as if I didn't have great Christmases. It's just that I was a little jealous. I always wished I wasn't alone."

"So you'll make sure you don't have just one kid—assuming you want kids…."

That topic was still a fresh wound and Nati had to force herself past the pain of it to answer him. "I do want kids and, yes, more than one. But not ten," she managed to joke.

"Yeah, I don't want ten, either."

"But you do want them?" It was none of her business. And she certainly shouldn't have any hope hanging on his answer—that was absolutely ridiculous.

And yet she realized that she did.

"I do want kids," he said. Which automatically made her like him even more. "Two or three maybe."

As a way to counteract his appeal Nati reminded herself that *having* two or three kids didn't necessarily mean that he intended to be an involved parent, though.

Cade finished his wine and set the glass on the coffee table. He pivoted more in her direction as he settled back, stretching an arm along the top of the couch cushions.

Nati had no idea why that slight repositioning made her even more intensely aware of his pure magnetism, but it did. And she couldn't help wishing that he would use that big hand that was so near to her shoulder to touch her…

"So none of you has produced the next generation of Camdens yet?" she asked to distract herself.

"Nope, not yet. It's something GiGi complains about."

Cade did reach for her then but it was only with two fingers to catch a strand of her hair. It was not what she'd been mentally urging him to do.

"I should probably take off," he said. "Tomorrow is still a workday."

"For me, too. I'll sand and polish your wall in the morning, and then it'll be finished," Nati told him.

Why did that make him frown?

"You'll work in the morning tomorrow? There's no chance you'll be there when I get home tomorrow night?" he asked, apparently for clarification.

"Morning," Nati confirmed. "Holly has a dentist's appointment in the afternoon so I have to watch both shops then."

His frown went darker. "What if I wanted to talk to you about doing another wall?"

"Do you?"

He smiled. "Maybe."

"Which wall?" she quizzed.

"I'm not sure."

"Well, I guess if and when you decide, you can let me know."

"But not tomorrow."

He sounded as disappointed as she was at the prospect of not seeing each other the next day. Which only reinforced Nati's conviction that it was for the best if they didn't cross paths. It was one thing to have talked herself into tonight. But as of tomorrow her work for him would be finished and that was a good time to end this tentative foray back into the dating world with him, too.

So she said definitively, "No, not tomorrow."

He sighed in resignation. "I had a good time tonight, though." His voice was quieter, and his eyes met hers while he still toyed with that strand of her hair.

"Me, too," she confessed.

He didn't say anything else, but kept looking into her eyes in a way that made Nati sure he was going to kiss her.

But instead he stopped fiddling with her hair and stood.

Slightly surprised by that, Nati watched him as he went to retrieve his sport coat from the bench. She watched him shrug into it, reveling in the sight before it occurred to her to get up and walk him out.

When they got to the door, she remembered to say, "Oh, don't forget your framboise."

"No, you keep it—I bought it for you. But thanks for sharing it with me."

"Thanks for buying it," she said, her own voice dwindling off.

They were standing facing each other in the doorway. All she could really think about was how beautiful his eyes were. How blue and warm and kind-looking with just a hint of devilishness to them.

He hadn't kissed her on the couch when she'd thought he was going to so she wasn't sure if she was reading the signals right this time, either.

Until he raised his hand to the side of her face, and gave her a featherlight caress.

Maybe she *was* reading the signals right.

"I keep wondering if your skin is as soft as it looks," he said in a throaty whisper as Nati tried not to melt into that scant massage. "It's even softer."

Then he tilted her face upward and slowly, slowly began a descent that she could have eluded.

Could have but didn't.

She saw Cade's lips part even before they met hers. Hers parted, too, and she was instantly caught up in a kiss that she'd secretly been dying for.

His other arm went around her and brought her in closer, close enough to deepen the kiss as his mouth opened wider, his tongue gently meeting hers.

His tongue—that was new. And nice. Nati let her head fall back farther still, raising her hand to his chest.

She pressed her palm to that wall of strong, solid muscle, absorbing the power hidden behind his sweater and sport coat before her hand rose to the side of his thick neck. The kiss rapidly grew more intense, their tongues taunting and teasing and playing a sexy game of chase.

Lost in that kiss, Nati wasn't sure when Cade had tightened his arm around her but she was suddenly aware of how securely she was being held against him, of her breasts nearly flattened to that expansive chest, of the fact that his hand had gone from the side of her face to her nape. She was suddenly aware of it all and of how her own body had melted into his, craving even more.

That's when the sound of the floor creaking above them intruded. Her grandfather was up and in his kitchen. Cade apparently heard the noise, too, because he retreated. The kiss cooled and finally came to an end.

Cade lifted his chin and rested it atop her head, leaving her cheek nestled against his Adam's apple.

But they only stayed that way for a moment before Cade sighed and eased his arms from around her.

Nati glanced up at him as they parted. He looked at her with a confused sort of mystery-man smile on those lips she hadn't had her fill of.

But he didn't say anything about the kiss. He merely whispered a gravely voiced, "Good night," before he reached for the door handle and opened the door.

"'Night," Nati whispered back, too shaken to be able to think of what else to say.

Then Cade walked out and she closed the door behind him.

The urge for more caused her to press her palm to the door as if that might somehow keep her in contact with him for just another minute.

Then she reminded herself that this wasn't—and couldn't be—anything.

Regardless of what every ounce of her might be calling out for.

Chapter Eight

"Finally! Pizza. I'm starving!" Nati said to herself when she heard the knock on her shop door at eight o'clock on Friday night.

She was in her workroom in the back of the store. Her hands were covered with paint, so she called out the workroom door, "I'll be right there," and went to the sink in the bathroom to wash up.

She'd had a full day. As planned, she'd finished Cade's wall in the morning. She could have done it in the afternoon because Holly's dental appointment had been canceled and Nati had been tempted to switch so she could be at Cade's house when he got home from work.

But the intensity of their kiss last night had unnerved her, and she'd resisted the inclination to rearrange her schedule. Even if he did hire her to do another wall or if she saw him in conjunction with his grandmother's hope chest, she knew that she should at least take whatever time she could as a cooling-off period. If she *could* cool off, because so far, the mere thought of that kiss heated her up instantly.

So in order not to make things worse for herself, she'd worked at his place in the morning, basking more than she should have in the sense of him there, in thoughts of the man himself, and certainly in the memory of that kiss that had rocked her world. Then she'd left his bill on the dining room table and slipped out.

As she left, she told herself that the best thing that could happen was for her to never see Cade again.

And she'd driven back to the shop feeling like that would also be the worst thing that could happen.

And fighting that feeling.

She'd been at the shop since then, trying to work off the pent-up desires that still tormented her from that kiss, from everything about the man, staying even after she'd closed up in order to get ready for the Scarecrow Festival the next day and the extra business she was hoping it would bring in.

She was still drying her hands on a paper towel when she headed for the front of the store.

But after taking one step out of the workroom, she could see through the glass in the door that it wasn't the pizza delivery boy knocking. It was Cade.

As a smile erupted on his handsome face at his first sight of her, Nati's heart literally fluttered. She liked this man too much, she realized in that instant. Much, much too much…

But he'd spotted her, he waved, and what was she going to do? She couldn't turn tail, run and hide, could she?

Of course she couldn't.

The problem was, she didn't think she could turn tail, run and hide from the feelings he inspired in her either.

Tossing the used paper towel into the trash as she passed by the counter, she unlocked the door and opened it.

"Hi," she greeted in a reserved tone of voice.

"Hi," he answered, looking at her as avidly as if he wanted to drink her in. "I probably shouldn't admit it, but I didn't have anything to do tonight so I thought I'd take a drive out here, see if maybe you were around. I can pay you and give you back these samples you did for the hope chest—" He held the samples up to show her he had them. "I went by your apartment and when you weren't there I thought I'd swing by here."

"I'm here," she confirmed. "I'm getting some extra pieces ready to put out for tomorrow in case the Scarecrow Festival gets me more foot traffic. I was getting everything ready."

Just then her pizza arrived, delivered by one of the waiters, who had walked it over from the restaurant.

Nati said hello and asked how he was before he told her how much she owed him.

Cade reached for his wallet. "Let me—"

"No," Nati said without hesitation, taking the money out of her jeans pocket to pay the waiter. "Keep the change."

The waiter thanked her and hurried off, leaving Nati holding the pizza box.

She raised it slightly and said, "Can I interest you in dinner or have you already eaten?"

"I haven't already eaten and that smells great, but I didn't come to mooch a meal off you."

"It's all right, I'll make you work for your supper—I could use a hand moving a couple of tables out front when we're finished."

"Deal!" he said as if the prospect thrilled him.

"It won't be fancy, though," she warned. "I was just going to eat out of the box—no plates, no silverware and paper towels for napkins. I do have some soda in the little fridge Holly and I keep but there's only paper cups."

"I think I can survive roughing it," he assured.

Nati cleared some space on one of her tables in the workroom and set the pizza box down. After getting them both drinks, she sat on one of the high stools next to Cade and they each grabbed a slice.

A few bites in, he said, "We need to talk about this bill you left me for the wall."

Nati responded with only raised eyebrows as she chewed and swallowed.

"It isn't enough," he told her.

"It's what I said I was charging you—materials and my hourly rate."

"Still, you had to drive across town to get there and gas is expensive—not to mention wear and tear on that old clunker of yours that I assume is still with the mechanic since I only saw the truck in your lot. I want to reimburse you for gas and mileage."

Nati shook her head as she finished her third bite of pizza, then said, "I don't charge for that. I've driven farther than your place for jobs before. Why would I expect you to pay for mileage?"

"Nati, this isn't enough," he insisted. "I saw the amount of work you did—it's worth more than this."

"I'm not Michelangelo painting the Sistine Chapel."

"Still, this was too many days of work, too many trips to and from my house. You did a great job, you didn't leave even a speck of dust for me to clean up after you—you've undercharged."

Nati rolled her eyes. "It's the going rate and what I bid, that's all there is to it. Are you complaining because I *didn't* overcharge you? Because if that's what you're used to because you're a Camden or something, you should take a harder line."

He laughed. "I just want to be fair and this isn't."

"It is if I say it is."

He shook his head and after finishing his second slice of pizza he wrote her a check. "I'm still including gas and mileage—consider it a bonus, or whatever you want."

Nati began to protest and he held up a hand to stop her. "No argument. I'm not used to having to argue to give someone *more* money."

He added that last part under his breath, as if it had special meaning to him that Nati didn't have to understand. But before she could say anything else the check was written out so she had no choice but to concede.

Plus she was a little distracted with just looking at him, taking in his khaki slacks and the way his long-sleeved hunter-green polo shirt hugged his broad shoulders and impressively muscled chest.

"Did your grandmother decide how she wants the hope chest done?" she asked as she picked up her pizza crust to finish it.

"She did. She likes the more antiquey-looking one rather than the brighter one you and I would have picked. I guess she wants the design restored but she wants it to look original."

"Okay, I can do that."

"And I'm still thinking about having you do another wall, but if you don't raise your price you're going to make me feel guilty."

"You *want* price gouging?"

"I *want* to be fair."

Nati rolled her eyes at him.

When they'd both finished eating, Nati went out to the counter to retrieve a jar of mints she kept hidden there. Those served as dessert. Then she put Cade to work.

"I just finished these tables so they need to go out front," she explained. "I was going to have to drag them but with two of us we can each lift an end and carry them. I have some new stock I want to display on them—some new punched tinware, and that set of plates, and those mugs, and all five of the teapots, along with the old campfire coffeepots. That will all go on one table. On the second table—" She pointed out the rest of the merchandise she'd painted especially for the festival, including doll furniture, two benches, a child's rocking chair and three toy boxes.

"You got all this done *and* did my wall?" Cade marveled when she was finished.

She would have accomplished even more if she hadn't spent as much time with him as she had. Or lost hours to daydreaming about him.

But she only said, "I did."

"Don't you sleep?"

Not as well as she had before she'd started to take images of him to bed with her, before she'd begun to replay his every word and relive every kiss.

But she wasn't going to say that, either. "I'm starting a business—I have to give it all I've got." And with that in mind, she added, "So let's move the tables—you take that end, I'll take this one."

The tables were both antiques. Nati had refinished them then added designs—she'd painted a border on the drop leaf of the round table, and stenciled a filigree in the center and at each corner of the rectangular one.

As they carefully maneuvered the first of them through the doorway that led to the front of the shop, Cade said, "So… Friday night and no date, huh?"

"I don't really date."

"You went out with me last night."

"Yeah, but… Well, that's the first time since before I was married. Since my divorce."

"And you were married to…"

He wanted to get into the meat of things tonight, did he?

But did she want to let him?

There were a lot of things she wanted to let him do but talking about her marriage hadn't been on the list.

On the other hand, maybe it was good to let him know where she stood.

So she decided to answer him. "I was married for six and a half years to a guy named Douglas Pirfoy."

"There are Pirfoys who own an airline—we had a contract with their freight division for air shipments for a while."

"Until the Camdens bought their own planes—I actually remember something about that," Nati said. The Pirfoys had been furious about the fact that the Camdens were also offering air shipment services to some of the Pirfoys' other customers and costing them business.

"I don't remember the name Douglas in any of our dealings, though."

"Doug. He's the heir apparent but he's yet to do more than look at the world as his playground. His father—"

"Eldridge?"

"Right. He's still in charge, and he claims that he'd like it if Doug would do more, but he also likes having all the power and calling all the shots, so he doesn't push it. In fact he indulges Doug like a kid and loves hearing about Doug's adventures, which only encourages Doug *not* to settle down."

"But he settled down to marry you…"

Nati laughed wryly at that. "Right. Yeah. Not so much."

"Uh-oh… He was a cheater?"

"No, actually, cheating was the one thing he didn't do."

"Because why go out for beer when you have champagne at home…" Cade muttered, looking over his shoulder as he walked backward with the table.

Nati wasn't sure she was meant to hear that and even though it made her smile she still had to refute it. "It was more like falling in love and getting married was an experience he'd already had. Since he only likes new adventures, new thrills, he was on to the next thing he or his friends could think of doing."

"Which left you where, in the scheme of things?"

Cade asked as they returned to the workroom for the second table.

"Home. Occasionally, he made a pit stop there, in between sailing a barge down the Nile and skydiving in the Amazon and sled racing in Alaska. The rest of the time, I was left alone with his mother trying to mold me into someone she would have *preferred* her son to have married."

"That doesn't sound good," Cade said ominously. "Where did you meet Pirfoy anyway?"

"College. I was at CU in Boulder on scholarship but to Doug it was just a great party town, so it was where he went to play when it was time for the college experience. He rarely went to classes—the school wasn't going to flunk him out when they were hitting his father for donations right and left. For Doug college was just about frat parties and girls and one wild excursion after another. Whatever he and his rich friends could dream up."

"If he didn't go to classes and you did, did you just cross paths on campus?"

"I had to work part time doing whatever I could—tutoring, babysitting, cleaning houses, dog walking, any odd job I could pick up. I met Doug when he hired me to waitress at an incredibly elaborate Gatsby-themed weekend in the mountains. Maybe it was the uniform I had to wear, but something about me that night sparked his interest. I figured he just wanted to diddle the help—"

"Diddle the help?" Cade repeated with a laugh.

Nati had overheard his parents use that term in reference to her relationship with their son. She shrugged.

"Whatever you want to call it, I turned him down. For the rest of our freshman year. Most of sophomore year, too. I suppose that made me too much of a challenge for someone like Doug to resist—"

"So he kept at it until he won you over."

"He's a charming, personable, attractive guy. And I'm only human—flying me to Maine for lobster, romantic picnics in places I would never have imagined—like on a mountain top that could only be reached by helicopter where he'd had a table and booth cut out of the snow, with a grill chef waiting to cook for us."

"Amazing…."

"Amazing me was one of Doug's specialties early on. And I was just…me. An only kid from a working-class family, getting swept off my feet by someone who could afford to do some mind-boggling sweeping. So yes, eventually he won me over—and not just because of his stunts, the stunts were just the backdrop for a guy who's intelligent and witty and clever and quick and really, really charming…."

Which she'd said twice now because it was so true.

"You're giving me an inferiority complex and making me wonder why you'd ever divorce a guy you still only have good things to say about," Cade complained as they went back and forth between the workroom and shop front with the merchandise that she wanted displayed for the festival.

Nati laughed because the idea of Cade being inferior to anyone—let alone Doug—was just plain funny.

"Remember, I was young and not nearly as worldly as Doug. I learned all too well that his charm was superficial, that there wasn't any substance behind it. But by senior year marriage was his next great frontier, so he kept at me about that. I held out for a while after graduation—almost a year."

"The time you spent working with the art restoration company."

"Right. And rather than going back to Philadelphia where he lived, Doug got an apartment here so he could still be with me. After a while…" Nati shrugged and said fatalistically, "I loved him and finally let him convince me to elope to Paris with him." Her voice had grown quiet. She busied herself with bringing out more of the merchandise from the back room.

"You eloped," Cade repeated, not letting her off the hook as he carried out the larger items. "No big society wedding?"

"I didn't realize it at the time, but I'm sure Doug knew that there was no way his parents would have been on board with him marrying me—they were *appalled* when they found out who I was."

"Who you were?"

"The daughter of truckers. The granddaughter of a housepainter. Not of their ilk—that was one of the nicer ways his mother put it when she was trying to teach me how to behave in 'their world.' Basically they figured I'd married their son for the money and that I was going to cost them. Which, I guess, ultimately, I did."

Cade glanced around her workroom as he picked up one of the benches to take into the front of the store. "This doesn't look like the lap-of-luxury from a big, fat divorce settlement…"

"I cost them money when my grandmother got sick four years ago with kidney disease. The medical bills were outrageous and my grandfather was going to have to sell his house. I asked Doug if we could help them out. He went to his father—because his father controls everything—and they did help, but the money was a loan and they expected my grandparents to pay interest."

Cade's eyebrows rose. "So let me see if I have all this straight—you married the heir apparent and got stuck spending more time with his nasty mother than with him, and when your family needed help the Pirfoys gave it but only as a loan?"

"Right. And then my grandmother died and I found out I was pregnant and things *really* got bad," Nati said with a sad laugh, remembering the nightmare she'd found herself in.

"Your grandmother dying was bad," he agreed. "But you getting pregnant was bad, too?"

"Doug couldn't have cared less—about either, actually. He didn't even come here with me when my grandmother was sick."

"You weren't living here?"

"Once we got married, we lived on the Pirfoy's estate back in Philadelphia. He didn't see any reason for us to have our own place when his parents' place was so big—plus it was another way for him to avoid taking any kind of responsibility—"

"So you were separated from your own family, too?"

"Completely. The Pirfoys didn't want to associate with them or even acknowledge that I *had* a family because they didn't come with a pedigree. I'd get back here to visit when I could but it wasn't as often as I wanted. And it definitely wasn't like living here."

"And he didn't even come here with you for…what? Your grandmother's *funeral?*"

"Doug was snorkeling with his buddies in Bimini. There was no way he was cutting that short for something as unimportant to him as my grandmother's funeral."

"Nice," Cade said venomously. "I'm surprised you didn't divorce him then—except you were pregnant…"

"Yeah. But then, when it came to a baby…" Oh, it had been months and months—why couldn't she say this without a catch in her throat?

Nati swallowed but still her voice was quieter when she went on. "The pregnancy was unplanned and when it came to a baby, when I told him I was pregnant, he shrugged and said, 'Okay, yeah, sure, a baby. If you want to have it, have it.' But he made sure I knew that it wasn't changing anything for him. A baby didn't fall into the category of adventure or a frontier to conquer."

"But there's no baby…" Cade said very, very carefully.

Nati kept from crying by focusing on setting up the display of hand-painted dishes. And not blinking. "No, no baby. I miscarried. Something else that Doug just shrugged off."

Nati took a deep breath that made her shoulders rise and fall in an elaborate shrug of her own and opted to get to the end of this conversation as quickly as she could.

"That was it for me. I couldn't spend another minute with his mother telling me how I dressed wrong, how I did everything below her standards, how I'd never 'be one of them' in order to have a mock marriage with a man I hardly ever saw, who couldn't have cared less about me. And my grandfather was grieving and I realized that this was really where I wanted to be. So I filed for divorce. That was when the real fun started." She also couldn't keep anger from her tone.

"I'm assuming that eloping meant no prenup…"

"No, no prenup—to Doug's parents' horror. But they had a whole league of high-paid, high-powered lawyers to come at me in spite of that and the Pirfoys held the paperwork on my grandfather's loan—their ace in the hole. I just wanted *out,* so that was my divorce settlement—my grandfather's loan was canceled and I came home."

"Oh, you made a *baaad* deal. For six and a half years of putting up with what you put up with, all you came out with was canceling a debt that shouldn't have been there in the first place?"

"I stayed with Doug as long as I did because I thought he would change. I kept thinking that he'd get the restlessness, the recklessness out of his system, that he'd go to work, and we'd end up with a normal marriage. I guess I just deluded myself. But he was my husband and I loved him. When we were together, when he wasn't off on some adventure, we were good together—"

"But after all that, to leave you nothing in the divorce is outrageous." The anger in Cade's voice won him points.

"Divorcing Doug—and the Pirfoys—was like a game of dodge ball where I was the only target. They and all their lawyers just kept throwing ball after ball after ball at me until all I could do was protect my head and huddle in the corner hoping to survive. I had lawyers even saying I was careless, that that's what had caused the miscarriage, that I'd been 'maliciously irresponsible' about my pregnancy, which was such a lie…."

"Of course it was," Cade said sympathetically and Nati just hoped he hadn't notice that her voice had cracked again.

She gathered some strength and went on, still genuinely trying to conclude this. "The first two lawyers I went to wouldn't even go up against the Pirfoys. The one who finally agreed to take me on was willing to do a David-against-Goliath thing. But when they threatened my grandfather over the loan, I just decided nothing was worth what they were putting us both through, so I took the settlement they offered and that was that—I chalked it up to experience."

Experience that told her loud and clear that she shouldn't go anywhere near another rich boy and yet there she was enjoying a glimpse of Cade's great rear end when he bent over to pick up the box of coffee and teapots he'd carried in and set on the floor.

He hoisted the box up onto the table so she could get to work arranging the display. The expression on his oh-so-handsome face was distressed.

"So, if your family had stayed in Northbridge and you'd gone to college there you wouldn't have met Pirfoy and—"

Nati laughed. "You keep going back to Northbridge," she observed curiously. "But that doesn't really mean anything to me. I just think that whatever happens in our lives is meant to happen. Even if it's hard to find a reason."

"It's hard to find a reason for this," Cade muttered.

Nati shrugged. “Regardless of everything else, if not for the Pirfoys paying my grandmother’s medical bills, my grandparents would have lost their house before my grandmother died. But that didn’t happen. That’s something.”

Cade laughed wryly. “And that’s enough for you? After six and half years of put-downs and neglect, after dealing with a nasty mother-in-law, after losing a baby?”

Nati didn’t want to—she couldn’t—think too much about the baby.

“I have my grandfather,” she said. “We have the house. I have Holly and now my own business—on the Camden scale that probably seems like nothing. But on the Morrison scale, we’re doing okay.”

Cade’s frown told her he wasn’t convinced but he didn’t say anything.

Once she’d finished arranging everything on the tables, Nati stood back to look over her work.

“I think that’s it,” she judged. “It took so much less time with help—thanks.”

“Just earning my supper,” Cade claimed as they both picked up the empty boxes and trays and returned to the workroom.

Cade deposited the boxes he was carrying in a corner, then pointed his chiseled chin in the direction of something a customer had brought to her that afternoon. “What is that?” He went over to it.

“It’s an old Victorian fainting couch. I need to redo the gold tip on the pattern carved in the wood around the upholstery.”

Cade straddled the bottom end of the couch and sat

down, bending over to pat the spot in front of him in invitation.

"Shall I swoon?" Nati joked, ignoring her better judgment to join him.

She sat facing him at the end with the sloping back. With one leg curved on the seat between them and the other foot remaining on the floor, she dropped her head against the upholstered slope and put her forearm to her brow.

"Somehow you don't seem like the swooning type," he said, reaching over to take her free hand to pull her upright. "But I do hate that you went through what you went through," he said quietly, holding her hand between both of his and rubbing the back of it with his thumb.

"But now it's time to move on. No more crying over spilt milk," she said dryly.

"Is there anything I can do to make things better? Can I invest in your shop, or help you get a place of your own, or a car? You still need a car…."

"Things are fine. They don't need to be better," she assured him. "My car will be fixed next week. My shop is in the black. And I like living close to my grandfather—I missed six and a half years with him, who knows how much longer I might have with him. Plus, my place might be small, but it meets my needs."

He shook his head as if he thought there was no reasoning with her but smiled a smile that hinted at admiration. "I do like a girl with pluck," he said. "And if we were still doing business with the Pirfoys we'd stop—how could I trust people dumb enough to let you get away?"

"Well, sure, there's that..." Nati joked, making him laugh.

Which was when it struck her that she didn't want to talk anymore. What she really wanted was for him to kiss her. That was what she'd really wanted since the moment she'd spotted him standing outside her door tonight. Or actually, since the moment he'd stopped kissing her the night before...

It was what made him so dangerous for her to be around.

But right now she didn't care. Her emotions were raw and she was a little in need of human comfort after talking about her experiences with Doug and his family. She just wanted Cade to kiss her...

He was studying her, searching her eyes, holding her gaze with his, but Nati wasn't sure he was getting the message.

Then he shook his head again and repeated, "Plucky..." as he tugged her toward him for the kiss she'd been waiting for.

Their lips met delicately at first. But it wasn't long before the kiss changed to something a whole lot more sensual.

Oh, she loved kissing him! He was just so good at it!

With her eyes closed, Nati drifted far into that kiss, into the pleasure of it as it gradually grew deeper, as their mouths relaxed and lips eased open more, as their tongues intertwined.

Cade slid closer to her. He let go of one of her hands and stroked the side of her face, his fingers combing up into her hair as the heat of his palm infused her cheek so wonderfully she couldn't help angling her head in that direction, into that caress.

Then he ran his other hand ever so lightly across her hip before running it down her thigh. He lifted her leg over his so he could move closer still.

A small, quiet voice in the back of Nati's mind told her to stop this before it went any further. But she just didn't want to hear it. Instead she raised her own hands—one to the column of his thick neck, the other to press to his chest.

She could feel muscle and power behind his polo shirt. And she liked that. Doug had been very thin, very lean, slight almost. But Cade had just the right amount of brawn to make him the essence of masculinity. And right there and then Nati drank it in and reveled in this man who was all man.

As their kiss deepened yet another level, Nati reclined against the backrest, lounging there, with Cade above her. His tongue tamed and taunted and teased.

She again ignored the little voice of caution in her head as things began to come awake, alive inside of her. Things that had been sleeping for a very long time. Yearnings. Yearnings for more. Yearnings to feel Cade's hand on more of her body. Yearnings to feel more of Cade beneath her own palms.

Her nipples were taut by then, making demands of their own that flooded her with even more desires. Her mouth went wide and she chased his tongue with her own, causing a rumble of laughter from his throat.

She found the hem of his shirt and insinuated her hands underneath it, laying them both on his broad back.

Skin. Oh, forbidden skin! Sleek and silky and warm

over more muscle, over sinews and tendons and broad, tight shoulders.

Nati reveled in the feel of his bare back, in running her hands along every inch of it and indulging herself in the purely primitive allure of skin against skin. Meanwhile, their kiss became an even more primal act.

Cade trailed his hand down from her cheek. To her neck. Her shoulder. Down her arm where merely the heel of his hand brushed the outer swell of her right breast.

It was almost nothing. And yet it was enough for her nipples to grow harder still, like twin diamonds that felt as if they might poke right through the tight camisole that served as a bra today.

Did he have any idea how badly she wanted his hand there?

He was still leaning over her, lost in that hot, steamy, plundering kiss, but their chests weren't touching so she doubted that he knew what he was arousing in her.

Then he covered her breast with his hand and he couldn't have been left guessing. Even through two shirts her nipple nestled into his palm.

With exactly the right pressure, the right firmness, the right everything, he kneaded her straining flesh, working it like a sculptor worked clay, sending waves of pleasure through her.

Oh, but he was good at that, too!

He reached his other arm over her head, resting it on the back of the fainting couch so he could come nearer, so he could kiss her even more soundly—if that were possible—while the hand at her breast slipped away to find a path under her shirts.

Nati couldn't muffle the tiny moan of delight when he did, when his fingers first touched her naked side, when his hand drew a tingling trail up to recapture her breast. It felt so good that she arched her spine and raised her other leg to drape it over his, leaving her straddling him, fighting not to writhe beneath the touch of that hand at her breast.

His hand worked a marvelous madness. Nati was carried away to a place where nothing existed but the two of them.

And yet it was at that moment that the little voice in the back of her mind somehow gained volume.

This wasn't the time. This wasn't the place. This wasn't a man she should be letting herself get carried away with….

And while she wanted to deny all of that, she couldn't. She'd just told him about what she'd gone through with Doug, with the Pirfoys, and in telling him she'd relived enough of the feelings to remind her of why she had to be cautious. She needed to be careful so soon after her divorce, but especially with a man who was even further out of her league than Doug had been.

It wasn't easy to deny herself. To call a halt to that kiss. To everything.

She had to, though. She knew that kissing, touching wasn't going to be enough if she let this go on much longer, and that making love with him there, on a customer's fainting couch in her workroom, was not something she could let happen.

So the first thing she did was place one of her hands over his where he touched her breast, stopping him in his tracks.

Then she ended the kiss, drawing away from him and opening her eyes.

"Maybe not the best idea," she whispered in a raspy, ragged voice.

She watched as Cade—eyes closed—drew a deep breath and with one final, longing caress of her breast, drew his hand out from under hers, out from under her shirts. Then he sat back and finally opened those brilliant blue eyes, nodding his concession as if he wasn't yet able to speak.

He curved an arm under each of her knees and lifted them, bringing them together in front of him. With her feet flat to the seat, nearly touching his crotch, he merely hugged her calves while he propped his chin atop her bent knees and smiled a bit blearily.

"I can't help myself when it comes to you, Nati," he confided quietly, as if it wasn't something he should be admitting to either of them.

He sat up straight and let go of her. Still straddling the fainting couch, he stood up and stepped over it.

"Come on, walk me out so you can lock up behind me," he said, holding out a hand to her.

She was so desperate to feel Cade's touch again that she didn't care if it was wise or not to take his hand.

He kept hold of her as they went from workroom to storefront to the door. Once they were there, he gazed down at her, his expression full of obvious disappointment that things had ended.

"So. The Scarecrow Festival—I'm thinking that sounds like fun," he said. "Any chance you can get away from the shop and tour it with me?"

Say no....

"Maybe," she said instead.

His smile broadened. "And who knows, I might even put in a bid on a scarecrow during the auction."

Nati laughed at that notion, not believing him. "Because it's what everyone needs," she joked.

"You never know."

Cade kissed her once more—a kiss filled with barely bridled passion—but cut it short. It wasn't soon enough to keep Nati from being swept up in the moment all over again though.

"Thanks for the pizza," he said in a husky tone.

"Thanks for the help," Nati whispered back.

With another kiss—this one chaste—he squeezed her hand and released it so he could open the door and go back out into the night.

And that was when Nati realized that she was standing there stiff as a board, willing herself not to want that man as much as she did.

While still wanting him so much she could hardly breathe…

Chapter Nine

"Sold! To the man in the turtleneck sweater!" the auctioneer called.

"I can't believe you did that," Nati said with a laugh.

She and Cade were outside of Arden's Old Town library early Saturday evening where the scarecrows were being sold to the highest bidders and he'd just bought hers.

"You're afraid of it," she reminded him, thinking back to his reaction to her scarecrow when he'd first come into her shop.

"It's grown on me," he claimed with a grin. "And I have the perfect place for it. Why don't you come home with me and I'll show you?"

Cade had arrived at her shop at three o'clock. For two hours he'd talked and joked around with both her and Holly. He'd encouraged customers to buy some of Nati's wares, and petted and played with the dogs of several of Holly's customers. He'd generally made those two hours fly by for both Nati and Holly, who was clearly charmed by him.

At five o'clock Holly offered to watch both shops for the last hour they were scheduled to remain open and encouraged Nati and Cade to go to the auction.

Now Cade wanted her to come home with him.

After what had happened between them in the workroom last night she'd been too wound up to merely go home and go to bed. In an attempt to work off some of that unexpressed energy, some of those unsatisfied desires, she'd stayed at the shop and worked until nearly four in the morning, completely finishing the design on his grandmother's hope chest.

She'd also spent that time telling herself that once the hope chest was finished, she could stop seeing Cade. That this could now come to a natural conclusion—exactly what she knew *should* happen.

In fact, she'd gone into today half hoping he wouldn't show up for the festival.

Of course the other half of her had spent the entire day watching for him and hoping he *would* show up, but such was her dilemma over the man.

Still, she honestly thought that the smartest thing she could do was get out of harm's way. She'd been firm with herself and made up her mind that today was the end. One way or another. That if he didn't show up, last night would be the last she saw of him, that she would even get the hope chest back to his grandmother during Cade's work hours next week so she didn't run any risk of seeing him again.

And if he did come to the festival, then today would be it.

Then she would put all her efforts into trying to forget she'd ever met him.

And kissed him.

And done more than kiss him.

She'd ignore the fact that she still wanted to do so much more that it almost burned her from the inside out....

Which was why she knew she should say no to going with him to his house now.

But somehow there didn't seem to be anything natural about concluding things right at that moment. In fact, it felt very unnatural. It felt cut too short. And she just couldn't make herself do it.

Plus she was curious about what he was going to do with the scarecrow. And it occurred to her that they could also load his grandmother's hope chest into the back of the shop truck and bring it with them, getting that out of the way. Then this truly would be the end of her association with the Camdens. Today. Tonight.

"I *am* wondering what you have planned for my girl," she said in a tone that was both intrigued and suspicious.

"Something good..."

"And since the hope chest is finished and you've already paid for the work, I could get it back to your end of town in the process—"

"And there's something else I want to tell you," he said, adding to the intrigue. "Something pretty big and important."

Nati arched her eyebrows in question but he shook his head. "Nope, I'm not telling yet."

"So I *have* to come?"

"You don't have to, but it would be good if you do."

The glint of mischief in his eyes increased her curiosity and made up her mind once and for all.

"All right. But this better be good," she threatened despite the fact that deep down she was thrilled to have found an excuse to spend a few more hours with him.

After loading the hope chest into the back of Nati's truck, Cade had strapped the scarecrow into his passenger seat and left Nati to finish closing up her shop and join him at his house a bit later.

Before she headed out, she went into the store bathroom to run a brush through her hair, and to freshen her lip gloss and blush.

She'd dressed today with the thought of seeing Cade so she was wearing her best, most expensive jeans, with a fit that was slimming and made her rear end look better than any pair of pants she owned.

To go with the jeans she was wearing a black lace knit shirt that also fit like a glove. The lining was flesh-colored, giving the illusion that she was showing more skin than she actually was. It had long sleeves, a square neckline, and a scalloped hem that barely reached the low waistband of her jeans. With the slightest movements, it exposed a hint of midriff.

Then Nati did the one thing that gave the outfit a little extra fire power—she took off the flat shoes she'd worn all day and slipped her feet into a pair of black suede heels she'd brought with her today *just in case...*

She shouldn't, she told herself when the mere feel of

the spiky three-inch heels made her feel like a new and much more daring woman.

Stick with the flats. They're frumpier. Safer. Tonight can't go where last night went....

But as good as her rear end looked in the jeans, the addition of the heels made it even better. It was the first time since her divorce that she'd ventured into spike-heel territory, and she just couldn't make herself go back to the frump. Not tonight.

"Watch yourself," she warned her reflection in the bathroom mirror. She turned around, craning her neck to get a look at her own rump and what the addition of the heels did to it, and then turned to face the mirror again.

She put on the black cashmere shrug she'd worn as a coat today and stuffed her flat shoes into her bag. Then she locked up the shop for the remainder of the weekend, and headed for Cade's house.

This one last time, she reminded herself.

Tonight and it was over…

"Okay, your dolly is back in the truck. I'll leave the hope chest in the entryway until Louie and I get it to GiGi's. Now you can come out back with me to see where your other creation will live."

"You put me in the backyard to literally scare away crows?" Nati asked as Cade led her from the entry to his kitchen and then ushered her outside.

"Not quite," Cade said in a self-satisfied tone.

Nati stepped out into the yard. She'd often gazed out at it through the dining room window when she'd been texturing his wall.

It was a beautiful yard—but not especially large. Well-manicured hedges lined the brick wall that acted as a fence. In the center of it all was a detached patio—a large square paved in slate with a brick fire pit, surrounded by wrought-iron chairs and tables and a love-seat-sized glider with fluffy cream-colored cushions. The entire patio was shaded by a redwood roof supported by vine-covered redwood posts. Along one side of the patio, there was an enclosed space containing a grill, an outdoor oven, sink and wet bar. The cooking and entertaining area put Nati's home kitchen to shame.

The scarecrow had been positioned in the enclosed area overlooking the fire pit. Nati also noticed that the stage had been set for tonight. There was a fire in the fire pit and a table near the glider had been set with plates, wineglasses, an open bottle of wine and take-out containers of food.

"Hmmm..." Nati mused. "Should I get out of here quick, before your guest arrives, or did you have more in mind for me tonight than delivering the hope chest and showing me what you did with my scarecrow?"

"I couldn't let you drive all the way over here just for that," he answered. "I thought we could have a little dinner out here with your doppelganger and enjoy the fire pit for the last time this season."

The whole scene *was* appealing—almost as appealing as Cade in his jeans and the heavy Irish fisherman's sweater he was wearing. And since Nati had already talked herself into this evening she just went with it.

"I *am* starving."

"Then let's eat," Cade suggested.

He led her to the food table, taking a piece of paper out of his pocket as they reached it.

"This restaurant had a write-up in the paper this week. Southwest fusion. I had to write this down to tell you what it all is," he explained.

He read from the paper as he opened each container. "This is slow-roasted pork shoulder with roasted corn puree and pumpkin seed sauce. These are lobster tamales with truffle puree and roasted pepper crème fraiche. These are chicken flautas. These are skewers of beef tenderloin, chorizo, bacon, peppers, grilled cactus, and cheese, in tomatillo salsa. This is guacamole with tortilla chips. This is something called queso fundido—it's a cheese dip. We use the little flour tortillas to eat it. And for dessert we have warm three-milk bread pudding with frangelico liquor, Tres Leches crème anglaise and blueberry compote."

Ah, the perks of a man who didn't live on a budget, Nati thought. But what she said was a simple, "Wow."

"I've never been to this place so I just said give me a couple of appetizers, something with fish, something with chicken, something with beef, and dessert, so I can't take the credit for having good taste. Or the blame if it's lousy."

"It all smells too good to be lousy," Nati assured him.

They each filled a plate. Cade poured the wine and then urged Nati to have a seat on the glider. They briefly sampled each of the dishes, gave their opinions and then settled in to eat, comfortable in the heat that came from the firepit.

As they were eating, Nati asked, "So what did you have to tell me?"

"Mmm-hmm," Cade said, putting a long index finger to his mouth to signal that she'd just reminded him but that he needed to finish his bite before he could answer.

When he had, he said, "First of all, the hope chest looks beautiful. GiGi will love it. And I'll take pictures of it to show Mandy as an example of your work."

"Mandy?" Nati repeated, hating the familiarity with which he said the name and, for some reason, instantly becoming suspicious. And jealous. Which she had no right or reason to be, she told herself firmly.

"Mandy Thompson. She's our decorator and you'll be hearing from her on Monday."

With her mouth full of succulent lobster tamale, Nati could only raise her eyebrows in question.

"I decided against having you do another wall here because something else occurred to me last night on the drive home. We just bought another office building—our executive financial and accounting department needed more space. It's in north Denver so it won't be quite as far to drive for most of our money people—or for you—"

"For me?"

"It's an old building that we've had to refurbish and remodel. Mandy is just starting to do the decorating and it struck me that it would be nice to have you texture one wall in each office."

"How many offices?" Nati asked.

"There's forty-two of them but I talked to Mandy this morning. I explained your shop schedule and the arrangements you make with Holly so you can fit in outside work. Mandy said she'll accommodate you. You two can hash it out together. She'll probably want something a little less elaborate than what you did on my dining room wall—there probably won't be plaster or sanding, just those other things you showed me where layers of paint look like marble or granite—so each office can be done in maybe one or two days. But there's no rush. If you need more time, individual offices can be vacated for a day or two even after we move in."

"Forty-two offices and you want a wall done in every one of them?"

"I do. I also told Mandy about your other work and she said she can always use someone good at stenciling and murals, too—Mandy is the decorator-in-demand around here and she does a lot of nurseries and kids' rooms on top of everything else, so she was excited to hear about someone who can do what you do. Plus she wants to look at the stuff in your shop."

Nati couldn't think of anything to say but another, "Wow..." because what he was describing—to become affiliated with a decorator—was tantamount to striking gold for her business all the way around.

Then, when it seemed almost too good to be true, she added, "Seriously?"

"You'll take the job?"

"I'd have to have my head examined if I didn't. This is a huge opportunity..." Then she heard herself say, "So this Mandy...you're close to her?"

Cade laughed. "Mandy is about fifty-five, she has a hulking husband, kids not much younger than I am, and if by 'close' you mean we've worked together before, then yeah, we're close. She does all the decorating for the Camden Incorporated offices, the lobbies. She did my house. If by 'close' you mean anything else, then no, we're not *close*."

"You haven't ever mentioned anyone else, and you said her name so…fondly…it just made me wonder…"

"If I said her name *fondly* it's because I like Mandy. She can be a little outspoken, but you get used to it." Then he smiled slyly. "But you were thinking she's what? A girlfriend? An old girlfriend?"

"I'm sure you have them," Nati insisted.

"Old ones, yeah. But no one more recent than a year and a half ago."

"How many *old* ones? Dozens? Hundreds?" she challenged, too curious not to persist now that she seemed to have a foot in the door on this subject that she'd wondered about since the minute they'd met.

"I haven't kept score of how many girls and women I've dated but I can't imagine that it's dozens —plural— let alone hundreds."

"How many stand out from the crowd?"

"Oh, I need dessert to talk about those…" he said, taking their empty plates and setting them aside. Then he went to the wet bar and fetched the single container that they'd left closed. After a moment, he returned to the glider with dessert and two clean plastic spoons.

"Let's see," he said. "There have been two affairs that stood out because they turned nightmarish, and two sort-of-serious relationships that seemed like they might go somewhere but then ended. One because I was barely twenty-two and wasn't ready to get serious about marriage the way she was. I guess your grandfather and I have that in common. The second ended because we both came to the conclusion that while we'd liked each other well enough to keep at it for over a year, we didn't really feel anything more than 'like,'" he said as he sat down again, at an angle to face her.

The spike heels might look fantastic but they pinched like vices so Nati kicked them off and shifted sideways to face Cade, tucking her bare feet under her hip.

Cade handed her a spoon and opened the container, setting it on the glider between them so they could share.

"So let's hear about the nightmares… I assume they were serious, too…" Nati prompted.

"They ended up serious. Ugly-serious," he said with some contempt.

They each tasted the bread pudding and rated it as delicious as the rest of the meal before Nati questioned him further. "Ugly-serious? What does that mean? Not an illegitimate child out there somewhere, because you said you didn't have any kids."

"Right, no kids. But with the most recent relationship that ended a year and a half ago, the woman claimed that I was going to."

"Uh-oh…"

"Yeah. We'd been seeing each other for about two months when she said she was pregnant and that the baby was mine."

"Was she lying?"

"She was pregnant but it wasn't mine. Of course by the time I could find that out with testing I was already in court facing her paternity claim. She demanded financial support throughout the pregnancy, child support and maintenance after the baby was born, plus a million-dollar settlement."

A third wow seemed in order so that was just what Nati said. "And the baby turned out not to even be yours?"

"Right."

Doug had faced his own false paternity claim during college, when Nati had still been resisting his attentions and had heard about it through the grapevine. So what Cade was describing wasn't a complete shock to her.

"The Pirfoys used to say that money and position made them targets for people who saw them as their payday. I thought it was cynical of them, but maybe not?"

"It isn't cynical. It becomes a reality you just have to watch out for. Try to avoid," he said solemnly. "Since the baby *wasn't* mine, nothing came of the lawsuit but the grief."

"Was your other ugly-serious relationship like that, too?" she asked.

"Oh, yeah. Even worse. It was a breach-of-promise suit." They'd finished dessert, so he put the spoons in the empty container and set it on the table.

"You made promises you didn't keep?" she said with a hint of sarcasm. Nothing she knew about him caused her to believe that that was something he would do.

"I did not," he said with authority. "I'd dated this particular woman on and off for about a year—she traveled for her job and we'd see each other when she was in town—no big deal. It was also no big deal when we'd go for weeks without any contact at all, either. Then she changed jobs, didn't have to travel, and we started seeing each other more often. Which was when I realized that I didn't really *want* a steady diet of her—"

"So you broke up with her."

"It really wasn't anything serious—when she was traveling we'd probably seen each other nine or ten times. And after a month of her being in town for good I knew it wasn't going to work out, so even though we'd sort of been together for a little more than a year—fourteen months to be exact—there had still only been a countable number of dates. But when I told her I thought we should go our separate ways, she filed a breach-of-promise suit."

"Just out of the blue?"

"Her claim was that she'd given me fourteen months of her life—at the height of her childbearing years. That I'd explicitly led her to believe I would marry her, that we'd talked about it—which we hadn't—and that she'd begun to plan for it by meeting with a wedding planner—"

"You went to a wedding planner with her?"

"No! No way! But she'd seen the wedding planner on her own and named me as her groom, so she thought the fact that the wedding planner was willing to confirm that aided her cause."

"That would look bad," Nati agreed.

"Jennifer also claimed that she'd changed jobs solely at my request because I hadn't wanted her to travel, because I wanted her to spend more time with me. And she'd told that to her previous employer when she'd quit. Since he didn't have any reason not to believe her—particularly when she was taking a lesser-paying job—he was going to testify to *that.* Basically, without my having any idea what she was doing behind my back, she was stacking the deck against me."

"And how much did she want in damages?"

"Four and a half million."

Yet another wow came out of Nati. "She wasn't fooling around," she added.

"No, and that one was actually harder to fight than the paternity suit. Paternity can be proven or disproven. It's a black-and-white thing—"

"But the breach of promise was he said she said."

"Her word against mine, yeah. If my lawyers hadn't had her investigated and discovered that I was the second guy she'd done this to, I could have actually lost that suit."

"The Pirfoys were very big on keeping to their own kind—there were a lot of reasons for it but one of them was to avoid people who were after their money—maybe you should take that into consideration," Nati suggested.

Cade smiled. "You're a cautionary tale from one side of the coin, I'm a cautionary tale from the other side. I guess we're both examples of how inequalities between two people in a relationship can leave one partner bearing a bigger brunt if the relationship ends. I know it's made me a little gun-shy..." he admitted somewhat under his breath.

"I understand that—I know I don't want my history to repeat itself," Nati agreed.

And with that in mind, she told herself this was the moment to put an end to being with Cade. Once and for all...

Even if she still didn't want to.

She took a deep breath, exhaled and said, "I should probably get going."

Cade studied her very intently, as if weighing how to respond to that.

Then he said quietly, "But I don't want you to…"

Nati pointed her chin in the direction of her scarecrow likeness. "The scarecrow and I are not a package deal," she joked.

Cade laughed. "Damn, I never even thought about making that a contingency."

"Too late now."

His smile turned more contemplative as he reached up to brush her hair slightly away from her face. "Cautionary tales… Why is it so hard to learn a lesson from them?"

"Good question," Nati said, thinking more about how close he was and the way the fire's dimming glow made him look dangerously attractive than about what she should be cautious of.

He touched her cheek, and she was so sure that he was going to kiss her that her eyelids dropped to half-mast in anticipation.

But he didn't. He went on studying her face, shaking his head again at something Nati couldn't fathom.

"You really are beautiful," he whispered, just before he did kiss her, but only lightly, chastely, a kiss that was more poignant than anything.

Nati knew she should have left it at that. Simple and sweet.

But without any premeditation, her head tipped to one side, she tilted her chin towards him, and the kiss became much more intense.

As it did, Nati wondered why there had to be such a battle between what the heart and body wanted and what the mind knew. Because her mind knew to just say no. To do what she'd intended to do—end things.

But now that she was with him everything felt so right, so good, so much like where she should be, that all her arguments seemed inconsequential…

His hand curved into her hair, cupping her head. The kiss found a new level of intimacy and still Nati didn't balk. Still Nati let her lips part even wider so their tongues could play with more abandon.

And suddenly her mind began to be won over to the side of her heart and body. This, tonight, with Cade, wasn't what she'd gotten into with Doug. It wasn't a commitment. It wasn't anything that could alter her entire life, her future. It couldn't cost her all that the Pirfoys had cost her.

This was just tonight. Right now.

Tomorrow would come and that would bring the natural conclusion to whatever it was she'd entered into with this man. But there wasn't anything natural about the end coming tonight. Now. Not when what he'd brought to life inside of her last night was reawakening by leaps and bounds.

And truly, what harm was there, she asked herself, in letting nature take its course until tomorrow? So what if she had one night with this incredible guy? Even if she was afraid that he could ultimately be bad for her, he wasn't bad for her for just this one night. Not as long as she made sure it wasn't for more than that…

She raised her hands to him—one to his chest, the other to his nape where she massaged his neck.

She wanted Cade. Maybe she'd wanted him from the first minute she'd seen him—there was certainly no denying that she hadn't missed a single detail, a single nuance of his appeal. Regardless, she wanted him now so badly that she knew she'd only been fooling herself to think she could merely say goodbye and never know him to the fullest extent possible.

She had to go to bed with him. She just had to. This once. She suddenly knew that there was no closure without it…

The fire was dying in the fire pit and the coolness of the October air was creeping in, tightening her already taut nipples almost painfully and sending chills along the surface of her skin that competed with the chills the kiss was causing.

So Nati brought the kiss to an end and whispered, "Inside?"

Cade's smile was tentative. "It was you who shut me down last night, as I recall, and I did not come into tonight with the intention of—"

"Neither did I," she said. "In fact I had every intention not to."

"But now you want to go inside?"

"Now I do," she said, leaving no doubt. "Unless you don't."

"You've gotta be kidding…" he said with a laugh that released all his pent-up frustration.

He took her hand in his and they stood up. Leaving everything behind—including her shoes—he brought her back into the house and straight upstairs to his bedroom. Once there, he swung her around and into his arms, instantly recapturing her mouth with an all new ferocity that Nati was only too willing to answer.

She raised both of her hands and held his head steady

for the kiss. His arms circled her waist and she felt the roughness of his thick sweater on her exposed stomach.

The wool was too rough on her bare skin, the sweater forming a barrier that was too thick between them.

So Nati let her hands course down his broad back until she found the sweater's hem. She yanked up on it, bringing it nearly over his head, then broke their kiss just long enough to rid him of it entirely.

For a moment she devoured the sight of his naked torso in all its magnificence, wondering only peripherally where a desk jockey got muscles like that.

He used the knuckles of one hand to lift her chin, raising her face to his. With a sexy, sexy smile, Cade sought out her mouth once more. As her hands traveled over each inch of his broad shoulders, his honed pectorals, his flat, flat belly, he tugged her lower lip between his teeth and taunted her with the tip of his tongue.

Nati kissed him back with every bit as much hunger, every bit as much urgency. She moved her palms along his sides to his back, following its ever-widening V to his massive shoulders. Then she drew her thumbs down either side of his spine, letting her fingers dip inside his waistband to where the curve of his rear end began.

At the same time, his hand finally traveled south, from her neck to her shoulder to her lace-covered breast.

Desire swelled her chest into his grasp but still it wasn't enough. Nati cursed all the lacy fabric that came between her skin and his touch.

But Cade wasted little time before bringing his hand around to her side and reaching under the scalloped hem of her shirt. His palm glided upward to cup her breast through her bra. Then he found his way past that, too.

His touch was as divine as it had been last night. Her nipple turned to a nib of oh-so-sensitive glass that strained for his every whim as he caressed and kneaded and massaged and manipulated her.

And still she wanted more. More. More. More…

Her shirt came off. Then her bra a moment later. Cade unfastened the button at her waistband, unzipped her jeans and slid those off, too, leaving her in only lacy bikini panties. He swept her into his arms and unceremoniously deposited her on his bed.

But he didn't join her there yet. As Nati again reveled in the superb sight of him, he rid himself of what remained of his clothes, giving her only a brief glimpse of just how magnificent he was before he came onto the bed with her.

He stretched out beside her and kissed her again, more slowly now, savoring it, savoring her, as his hand found her breasts—first one, then the other, in tender squeezes that seemed to keep pace with the beats of her heart and only built the anticipation.

Then his mouth trailed to her breast. He was tender at first, then more insistent as he sucked her nipple far into the dark cavern of his hot, moist mouth and circled and flicked that tight crest with his tongue.

While he did that, his hand traveled down her stomach to slip between her legs.

Nati couldn't keep from writhing as his long fingers explored and found entrance. He drew them in and out slowly.

She reached for him in turn without much preamble. He was long, thick and unyielding; the majesty of him only increased her desire.

Shifting onto her side, she brushed one of her legs up against his thigh. She could tell that she was getting to him, too, because a low rumble sounded in his throat.

Then everything stopped for a moment while he rolled away to his nightstand and found protection. When he returned, he kissed her again with a languid hunger, then came down on top of her and insinuated himself between her pliable legs.

It was such a wonderful weight, to have him there above her.

Nati's arms went up and over his shoulders, her hands pressed to his back, as he came fully into her with slow purpose.

Nature really did take its own course from there as they moved together in perfect cadence. Perfect, rhythmic cadence that swept Nati into a world where there was only Cade and the feelings, the sensations, he was bringing to life within her. Feelings and sensations that got stronger and stronger, building, growing, getting bigger and better with every thrust.

Faster and harder he plunged until Nati couldn't keep up any longer. She could only hold tight to him as wave after wave washed through her, lifting her higher and higher until she was held aloft in the golden glow of an unbridled ecstasy that she'd truly never experienced the likes of before.

She knew she was digging her fingers into Cade's back but she couldn't help it. Her own back came away from the bed, as every inch of her froze in that sublime surge of passion and pleasure that sent a small, high-pitched sound from her arched throat. Every muscle in

Cade's body tensed and froze, too, letting her know that he was reaching a peak of his own.

He pressed deeper and deeper into her—so far that it wasn't possible for him to press any farther, embedding himself in the core of her. They were melded together in a way that Nati wanted never to end even as it began to. As her own body began to relax and concede exhaustion. As the curve in her spine, the arch of her neck eased and laid her flat to the mattress again. As Cade started to breathe and unwind, to rest more of his weight on her.

For a moment they both stayed that way, basking in the aftermath, their bodies molded perfectly together.

Then Cade pushed his upper body away from her to rest his forearms on either side of her head, and kissed her brow. "I swore I was going to behave tonight," he confessed.

"Me, too," Nati answered with a tiny laugh.

"You just get to me, you know?"

The same way he got to her. "I'd apologize but you get to me, too."

He smiled a weary smile and kissed her on the mouth before he said, "I'd like to get to you a whole lot more."

Nati laughed again.

"Will you stay?" he asked as if everything in his life depended on it.

"I don't think I could drive home," she admitted. Her lack of sleep the previous night and what they'd just indulged in had caught up with her.

"So if I just keep you exhausted you'll never leave? I think I can do that," he said with laughing insinuation as he slipped out of her and rolled to his back. He pulled her over to lie close beside him, both of his arms wrapped tightly around her.

And in the warmth of that embrace, her head pillowed by one of his pectorals, Nati could no longer resist slumber.

But even as she gave in to it, she was thinking about Cade, about what they'd just done, about the intentions she'd brought with her tonight and then discarded.

Yet in those few minutes right before sleep took her she knew without a doubt that even though she had gone against every vow she'd made to herself, it had been worth it.

Chapter Ten

"I'll admit I was hoping to find out that leaving Northbridge was the best thing that ever happened to the Morrisons," GiGi told Cade on Sunday as the two of them sat in GiGi's kitchen making a salad. "Which doesn't seem to be the case."

No one else had arrived for dinner yet. Cade had come early in order to tell his grandmother that his mission with the Morrisons was complete and what the outcome had been.

"But," the elderly woman continued as she stood up, "I'm at least glad to know that they did all right, that Jonah had a good and happy life, that he's happy now. And I appreciate that you found a way to help his granddaughter become a success from here on—working with Mandy ensures that she'll do *very* well."

On her way to the refrigerator for more salad fixings, GiGi paused to kiss Cade on the cheek.

"Thank you. You did exactly what I wanted and now you can go back to business as usual," she said.

Cade had no idea what there was about his expression that gave him away. But one look at his face and his grandmother reared back, raised her eyebrows and said, "Unless you don't want to go back to business as usual. Maybe you like this girl…."

His report to his grandmother had been like any business report. He'd stated facts, tracing the repercussions of what H.J. had done in foreclosing on the Morrisons' farm in Northbridge through the generations. He had not said anything about what had happened between himself and Nati personally. Certainly he hadn't told his grandmother that Nati had spent last night with him. That they'd made love repeatedly. That Nati had somehow managed to slip out before dawn this morning without waking him, without leaving so much as a note, and that he'd been in one hell of a quandary ever since.

But apparently just like when he was a kid, GiGi could see right through him.

"*Do* you like this girl?" his grandmother asked.

"She's…great," he said. It was the truth, even though he said it with reservation in his tone.

Sensing his hesitation, his grandmother said, "But she doesn't have much on her own. Jennifer and Aggie didn't have much on their own so they were angling for a way to soak you."

"But *un*like Jennifer and Aggie, Nati is as honest as the day is long," Cade said, denying there was any similarity among the three women. "I tried to talk her into raising her prices, they were so low. I couldn't even get her to charge mileage for coming across town to my house. And she's already experienced the perks of money through marriage. But rather than fighting tooth and nail for anything in her divorce, she settled for a pittance. Hell, she didn't even expect me to pay for everything when we were together—*she* bought *me* ice cream and pizza."

"So she's not like Jennifer and Aggie," his grandmother concluded. "But do you think she might have some kind of secret axe to grind because of who you are?"

"I poked around at that issue more than once," Cade said. "Her reaction was always the same—there was no anger. She believes that the way the Morrisons' lives played out was the way they were meant to play out."

"She's an upstanding person who doesn't seem to want anything from you—or us," GiGi summarized. "She's 'great,' but…what? You just don't like her?"

Cade laughed, though it was wry and pained because to say that he didn't like Nati was so far off base. The truth was that he liked her too much. So much that it really did worry him.

What if he'd missed something the way he'd missed seeing the other women for what they were? Those two storms had been tough enough to weather. But with Nati? He didn't know what he'd do if he was wrong about her. He didn't know if he'd survive…

Somehow his grandmother sensed that, too.

Sweeping by him on her way back from the refrigerator, she pinched his cheek. "My big strong grandson is mush for this girl and shakin' in his boots, isn't he?" she said with a laugh of her own.

Cade scowled at her.

"Those two little gold diggers knocked you for a loop, Cade. They bruised your poor fragile male ego and now you're just not sure someone will want you for you."

"I don't think I'm quite that delicate," Cade scoffed. "But how the hell *am* I supposed to be sure a woman doesn't just want me for the money unless the woman has money of her own? It didn't even occur to me before Jennifer's and Aggie's antics that it was something I had to watch out for."

His grandmother smiled a serene smile as she sliced carrots. "Maybe that's my fault. I tried to raise all of you kids to be humble, to believe that you weren't any better or worse than anyone else. I didn't think to teach you that folks who have less than we do could be a threat. Maybe I should have taught you to be more suspicious. But still, now you just have to trust—yourself, Nati, your own instincts—"

"The instincts that failed me twice now?"

"The instincts that tell you if a person is right or wrong for you—you knew Jennifer was wrong for you, that's why you broke up with her. You didn't have any way of knowing that she was plotting behind your back and that breaking up with her gave her an open door for that breach-of-promise suit. And even with Aggie—you'd only been going out with her for a short time, it was nothing serious until she made it that way by saying you were the father of her baby. You might not have had the instinct to run yet, but you also weren't completely sold on her, either."

That was all true enough.

"What do your instincts tell you about Nati Morrison?" GiGi asked as if she already knew the answer.

Still, Cade thought it over, really exploring what he knew of Nati before he said, "That she's genuine and unaffected, which makes her a little like you," he admitted. "That she's sweet and kind and honest and good-hearted and hard-working and—"

"And she's beautiful—oh, what babies the two of you would have!"

Cade rolled his eyes. "*Was* this just some matchmaking thing you had up your sleeve?"

"How could that have been?" GiGi said a bit too innocently. "I'd never even met the girl."

"But you'd talked to that friend of yours who had hired her before. Did you know more about Nati than you've let on?"

GiGi merely smiled. "It's not me we're talking about now. It's you. And the fact that you like Nati Morrison. More than a little, maybe..."

Waking up this morning to find that she wasn't in bed with him had left him with an empty feeling. And since then he'd missed her so much it nearly had him doubled over. There wasn't any doubt—he liked her more than a little.

"It's all so awkward," he complained. "You and your old flame—how is that supposed to work?"

"Just fine," GiGi said calmly. "Don't let me and my *old flame* stand in your way."

Was she hoping that Cade's getting together with Nati would bring Jonah Morrison back into her life?

It made him wonder if he was seeing through his grandmother a little, too.

GiGi broke into his reverie before he could be sure. “For what it’s worth, I say just think about this girl—separate from the others, separate from any thoughts of money. Just think about the girl and how you feel about her. Then go with your instincts, Cade.”

The elderly woman took the salad to the refrigerator and added, “Now I want to put on a little lipstick before everyone gets here so I’ll leave you to it.”

Which she did, abandoning Cade to the big empty kitchen with only his thoughts of Nati.

But there wasn’t a whole lot of thinking he needed to do, he realized within moments after his grandmother had left.

When he thought about Nati purely in her own right, he didn’t suspect her of gold-digging. She might not have much, but she’d already proven that money and material wealth weren’t what was important to her. What was important to her was her family, her friends—the same things that were important to him.

And when he thought about the way he felt about her?

If they weren’t so right for each other they wouldn’t have come as far as they had, as fast as they had. He wouldn’t have spent every minute he was away from her since they’d met thinking about her, daydreaming about her, just wanting to be with her again. He wouldn’t have felt as if a part of him was missing every minute they were apart. He wouldn’t have so completely lost sight of everything and everyone else whenever he was with her, as if she was the world for him.

The absolute truth was that money—his having it, her not having it—didn’t matter.

What was important was that the minute they'd met it was as if everything had fallen into place. They were just two people who fit together seamlessly. In bed and out of it. It was a rock-solid foundation from which everything else could blossom—a life together, kids, everything that old H.J. had built his empire for. They were just two people who made each other happy.

In fact, she made him happier than he could ever remember being. He thought—he hoped—that he made her equally as happy.

He knew that he wanted to keep making her happy—and money didn't factor into it. For them, happiness would be about so many other things; the money was only incidental.

He wanted to spend every minute of the rest of his life with her. He wanted never to wake up another morning—like he did this morning—without her.

And he didn't know how he was going to get through Sunday dinner without telling her that…

He left the kitchen and stood at the foot of the stairs.

"GiGi? I'm not staying for dinner," he called.

"You know how I feel about that," his grandmother yelled back in warning. "Sunday dinner is mine."

"I can't help it. I have to go."

There was a moment's pause before GiGi called down, "I'll set a place for her next week…"

Cade laughed as he turned and nearly ran out the front door.

Top to bottom, inside and out, Nati's apartment was spotlessly clean. Cleaning it had occupied every minute since she'd slinked home from Cade's house just as the sun was rising. Cleaning was what she did to regain her balance when things felt as if they were spinning out of control.

She'd come awake at five this morning. Naked, snuggled against an also naked Cade, wanting him for the fourth time as badly as she'd wanted him the first. And wondering if there was a way to stay right where she was for the rest of her life.

That was when she'd realized that things were spinning out of control.

And it terrified her.

Out of control, vulnerable and helpless—that was how she'd felt during her divorce. It was how she'd felt until only recently. Now she was feeling that way all over again.

So she'd eased herself out of Cade's arms, out of his bed, and snatched her clothes to dress in the hallway. Then she'd slipped out of his house in too much of a hurry to retrieve her shoes from the patio, driving home barefoot.

She'd arrived before her grandfather was up and could see her walk of shame. Right away, she'd thrown herself into frantic cleaning, spending the day purposely reliving the worst memories of her marriage, of her miscarriage, of her divorce, in order to remind herself why she could not give in to her growing feelings for Cade Camden.

A hot shower and a nearly punishing shampoo ended the afternoon. Then, dressed in gray and pink pajama pants and a warm long-sleeved T-shirt, she decided she'd better at least have a piece of toast since she hadn't eaten all day. She was just going to the kitchen when there was a knock on the outside door to her apartment.

If it had been her grandfather he would have used the inside door at the foot of the steps to the basement.

It might be Holly.

Nati had called Holly this morning. She knew that Holly was spending the day with her parents and that they had a no-cell-phone policy during their visits. When Nati had reached voice mail she'd left a quivery message that she needed to talk to Holly later. She hadn't heard back from her, but it would be like Holly to recognize the distress in her voice and just show up.

Really, really hoping that it was Holly, Nati went to the door and opened it.

But it wasn't Holly.

It was Cade.

Which, in Nati's state of mind, was the worst-case scenario because just one look at him standing there tall and handsome, dressed in jeans and a cashmere crewneck sweater, made her want to throw herself into his arms all over again.

But she didn't. She held fast to the doorknob and whispered an apprehensive, "Cade…"

"Hi," he said, somehow managing to infuse that single word with warmth and comfort and understanding. "I'm not who you wanted to see, am I?"

There was no sense pretending any differently so Nati gave him a dour shake of her head.

"I know. The whole way over here I thought about things from your perspective and I finally figured out why you left the way you did this morning."

Oh, she didn't want her grandfather to overhear that!

If the window directly above her door was cracked even slightly and Jonah was at his sink, he would.

She put an index finger to her lips as she stepped back, allowing Cade inside, all the while keeping her distance from him.

She didn't ask him to sit down. She didn't offer him anything to eat or drink. She merely stood there, wishing like mad that he didn't look—and smell—so fantastic. That she didn't want him the way she did.

He closed the door and came closer, but not too close, before he went on.

"Initially I thought that I'm probably your first since your divorce and maybe that shook you up. Then it occurred to me that this wasn't about sleeping together..." He held both hands out, palms up, moving them like scales weighing two evenly matched quantities. "Pirfoys, Camdens, to you I probably seem as treacherous as Doug Pirfoy was."

"More." The word came out on its own.

Cade nodded, studying her, so sympathetic she thought he could see her fear.

"To be honest," he said, "until just a little while ago, I had my own stuff from the past to hash out, too. But you don't have anything to do with that. I needed to keep you separate, to just think about you, who and what you are. And when I did that, I knew I was wrong to ever lump you in with anyone else. What we have together—and can have together—is something completely new."

He went on to say good things. Wonderful things. About Nati. About what he wanted from now on.

"I want you, Nati," he finally said point-blank. "It already feels like I've known you forever. Like you were just out there, made for me, and waiting for me to finally find you. You and I are supposed to be together—I'm so sure of it that I can feel it all the way to my bones."

Oddly enough, that didn't come as a surprise to Nati because she felt it, too.

Which only made it all the more difficult for her to stand her ground.

But she had to. He was still who he was. And she'd had the day to relive the lessons she'd learned. Lessons that had left her scarred and scared. That had led her to the conclusion once and for all that Cade was like her food allergy—no matter how incredibly good the strawberries might taste, if she ate them, she'd break out in hives, she wouldn't be able to breathe, and she might not live through the indulgence.

"I'm sorry," she said. "But I've been down this road before. And I know you mean what you're saying right now. But I also know about people who are used to getting what they want, who can have anything they want, do anything they want. I know that they just keep wanting something else and doing something else, that—"

"That was your ex—"

"And all the friends who lived the same kind of life he did—"

"But it isn't me," Cade insisted. "I get up every morning and go to work like everyone. I work five days a week. I have dinner with my family every Sunday. I'm not Doug Pirfoy looking for the next thrill or the next mountain to climb or the next conquest—"

"The next conquest is what your whole family history is about," Nati said. "Building, expanding, taking over—you wouldn't be where you are without it."

"Okay, in business, sure, but that's just business and it's not what I'm out looking for every minute of my life. It's not me as a person. I'm not all about the next challenge or thrill. I'm just what you've seen of me—I want to be with you, come home to you, wake up with you in the morning, live an ordinary life with you—"

"An ordinary life," Nati scoffed. "Maybe for now. But the rest of the time? I know better. An ordinary life isn't having your name in the newspaper every other day. It isn't hanging out at a country club where only the elite are allowed. It isn't charity galas, and the private planes I'm sure you have at your disposal, or the army of people I'm also sure are at the ready to grant your every wish and whim just because your name is Camden."

"Yeah, sure, all of that is there, Nati. But you need to judge me separately from it. You need to judge me separately from the ex-husband who happened to live like that, too. I'm just looking at you," he said, his cobalt-blue eyes steadily on her. "And I need you to just look at me, to let the rest of it fade away and just see me!"

She did just see him and it was every bit as amazing a sight as it had been since that first day in her store. And it made her eyes flood with tears for no reason she could fathom.

"I see you and a huge family that's ultimately only loyal to you, and a legion of lawyers that I'd have to come up against if it didn't work out," she said. "And I can't be the little guy going up against the giant again. I can't be in a place where some perfect *stranger*—some lawyer—is telling me that I did something wrong and that's why I lost my baby. I won't be." Her voice cracked and she could no longer prevent those damn tears from escaping, and she hated that all she wanted was for him to put his arms around her and hold her.

"Nati..." he said so sadly, stepping towards her, his arms out to do just what she wanted him to do.

But she stepped back, out of his reach.

"No," she said as firmly as she could from behind the tears. "I'm just getting my life back together. I won't let it be swallowed up by the Camdens the way I got swallowed up by the Pirfoys—"

"I'm not asking you to do that. I'm just—"

"No! We're done. Last night was...it. It was the end. It was all there's going to be."

Nati shook her head, fighting not to sob. She gave him a wide berth as she went back to the door and opened it.

"We're done," she insisted in a voice that was soft and sorry but left no doubt that she meant what she said.

"No."

"Yes."

She opened the door even wider to let him know she wanted him to go.

For a long time he didn't. Nati could only look at the floor because she was too afraid that one glance at him would sink her resolve.

Then, in a low, gravely voice, he said, "This is wrong. We belong together..."

"It's not going to happen," she said.

"Because you're not letting it happen," he accused.

"No, I'm not."

Another moment passed before he finally walked out of her apartment.

And that was when Nati really broke down.

Chapter Eleven

"This is kind of outside your usual territory..." Nati observed from the passenger seat of her grandfather's car.

It was Friday night and Jonah had insisted that Nati let him take her out—first to dinner at his lodge, then somewhere else that he said was a surprise. Since his retirement he rarely ventured too far from Arden but here they were now, on the highway headed for downtown Denver.

"I can still get around," he said as if she were challenging him. "I used to cover all kinds of territory when I was painting houses."

"I know, but I just thought my surprise would be ice cream or a movie or something..."

"You're too far down in the dumps for ice cream or a movie to lift your spirits. Holly and I have been trying things like that all week and it hasn't helped."

"I'm sorry," Nati said, recognizing that both her grandfather and her best friend *had* been rallying around her since Sunday's fiasco with Cade. Nothing had helped. The truth was that she somehow felt even worse over things coming to an end with Cade than she had when she'd finally gotten through her divorce.

"I don't know why it is," she went on, "with the divorce there was some sense of relief, but this… It's dumb. It was nothing with Cade and here I am—"

"Holly and I can both see that it wasn't *nothing,*" her grandfather said as he exited the highway and then drove along Spear Boulevard into the Cherry Creek area. "We think there's even more here than there was with Doug—"

"I *married* Doug."

"But you wouldn't even go out with him for the first year he chased you. This one… With this one, there's a lot more or you wouldn't have been so red, white and blue."

"I've been patriotic?" Nati asked, confused.

"Your eyes have been red from crying all the time, your face is as white as a ghost, and your mood is more blue than I've ever—*ever*—seen it."

Nati laughed weakly, "Ah, I get it—red, white and blue. I didn't realize I was such a mess." That was a lie; she was actually more miserable than she'd even let her grandfather or her friend know. But she'd been doing her best to hide the evidence of the river of tears she'd cried this week and the fact that she could barely eat or sleep.

Jonah reached over and patted her knee. "Don't worry, you were still the best-looking woman at the lodge tonight. But look at you—black pants, a gray sweater—you look like you're in mourning. And Holly and I can see how sad you are," he said as he turned off Spear onto a street that Nati suddenly recognized.

Things got more alarming when he pulled into the drive that led up to the Camden family home.

"What's going on?" Nati demanded.

Jonah came to a stop at the front of the house and turned off his car engine, removing the keys from the ignition before he said, "Georgianna called me."

That *was* a surprise.

"Oh, no..."

"It's all right. It was nice. We had a long, long talk. We cleared the air, we laughed, we reminisced—it was really good."

Nati glanced over at her grandfather. Was there an underlying affection in his tone? "You didn't mind talking to her?"

"An hour and a half on the phone, like two teenagers—it was fine."

Or maybe better than fine?

But Nati didn't have the oomph to get into that. Besides, there was something more pressing—they were parked in front of Georgianna Camden's house!

"What are we doing here?" she asked, taking only slight comfort in the fact that there were no other cars in sight so it was unlikely that Cade was also there.

"Georgianna asked me to bring you. She wants to talk to you." And as if that put an end to any discussion, Jonah got out of the car.

Nati had a bad feeling about this.

But what was she going to do, sit there like a stubborn child and refuse to go in?

Cade's car isn't here, she told herself.

Maybe the elderly woman just wanted to talk to her about the hope chest. Maybe she hadn't liked the work Nati had done on it.

Even though she knew it was crazy to be wishing for a complaint about her work, it was preferable to anything else the other woman could have to say to her.

She got out of the car for her grandfather's sake, but not without saying, "I don't like this," as they went up to the front door.

It opened before either of them had gotten anywhere near the doorbell. And there stood Georgianna Camden in a casually snazzy little outfit of gray slacks and a mandarin-collar tunic. Nati had the impression that GiGi had dressed up for her first meeting with Jonah after so many years.

Maybe I'm just the excuse they used to see each other... Nati thought as she stood aside and watched their reunion. The two clasped hands and exchanged a warm greeting filled with compliments about how handsome Jonah still was and how Georgianna was even more beautiful after all these years.

When they'd finally fawned over each other long enough, only reluctantly releasing each other's hands, Georgianna Camden turned to Nati and greeted her with a hug that Nati didn't see coming.

"I asked Jonah to bring you," the older woman said. She locked elbows with Nati, guiding her and Jonah into the formal living room where she urged them both to sit and then sat herself—on the elegant coffee table in front of the sofa, as casually as if they were in a cabin in the woods rather than a Cherry Creek mansion.

"My grandson is crushed," she said then. "He's putting up a good front, but I've never seen him as unhappy as he's been since you showed him the door last Sunday."

So she knew....

Nati had no idea what to say to that.

Georgianna continued before she could respond anyway.

"It took some bullying, but he finally told me what happened between the two of you and why you don't want any part of him. Or us. And that's when I knew I had to give you a little talking to."

And there Jonah was, sitting beside Nati with a delighted smile on his face, as if he just couldn't keep his eyes off the older woman.

Nati wondered if lack of food and sleep this week had put her into some kind of coma and maybe she was just dreaming this whole thing.

"Cade also told me about you and the Pirfoys," Georgianna said. "Believe me, I know plenty of people like that, but I'm here to tell you that I'd kick any one of my grandchildren right in the seat of the pants if they behaved like your ex-husband did."

Georgianna leaned forward to confide, "I'll tell you the truth, after those two gold diggers tried to squeeze Cade and he told me he was only sticking to women who didn't need his money I worried about what he might bring home. The last thing I want is some snooty little debutante as a granddaughter-in-law."

Or maybe I'm just punch drunk, Nati thought when that made her laugh.

"This family has money," Georgianna went on. "There's no denying it. It's a fact. But no matter what, the family comes first. Believe it or not, it was even like that with H.J., in his own way."

The silver-haired woman cast a glance at Jonah then went back to focusing on Nati. "Your grandfather and I had a long talk and he understands that even all those years ago, when H.J. took over the mortgage on the Morrison farm in Northbridge, it was, in H.J.'s way, an act of love. Hank had his heart set on me and H.J. was too afraid that if he didn't put some distance between me and Jonah, I might choose Jonah instead of Hank. And Hank's happiness was the most important thing. Cade's happiness is one of the most important things to me. And you are the key to Cade's happiness."

Nati still didn't know what to say.

"He's a good boy, my Cade," Georgianna said, not seeming to need any response from Nati. "And you don't have to worry that he'll let anything or anyone come before you, or that once he has you, he'll put you on a shelf like a toy he's lost interest in. I'd shoot him myself if I saw him act like that. But that's just not who he is. And yes, I understand you're worried that you'll get swallowed up by us. I'll admit to you that that's what happened to me when I first married into the Camden family. That's why I wanted to talk to your grandfather and get you both here tonight..."

Georgianna smiled at Jonah before turning back to Nati.

"Your grandfather has forgiven me for what was

done way back when, and we agreed that if you became a part of this family, your grandfather would come right along with you. In fact—"

Yet another glance was exchanged between the elders, yet another smile that made Nati even more suspicious that something had been rekindled between them.

"I'd expect Jonah for Sunday dinners every Sunday right along with you," Georgianna said. "Your friend Holly—Cade told me about her—she'd be welcome every Sunday, too, just the way any friend of any of my grandchildren is welcome. The more the merrier—that's always been the policy around here. When I left Northbridge I felt isolated from my own family—I'm guessing you felt that way living in Philadelphia—and I didn't like it. Family is family—I'd treat all your relatives like they're my own. And I hope that you'd do the same. I'd even get my feelings hurt if you had some shindig and didn't include me."

Nati smiled, imagining Georgianna Camden whooping it up in her little basement apartment.

The older woman sighed and frowned then, as if she didn't like the next part of what she had to say.

"Jonah filled me in on what you went through divorcing those airline people," she said then. "There were certain similarities between the way they treated you and the way the Camdens treated the Morrisons."

Nati glanced sideways at her grandfather. "You had a lot to say," she said with some surprise.

Jonah shrugged.

"Those kinds of things would never go on now," the elderly Camden continued. "What we give, we give freely. It does not come back to bite anyone in the backside. And I can promise you that if you and Cade got together and—God forbid—something happened that put an end to it, that would be between you and Cade. It wouldn't be you against the lot of us. You might not believe it after tonight, but I stay out of my grandchildren's business."

Georgianna smiled as if she saw the humor in her own claim but she didn't belabor the point. Instead she took both of Nati's hands in hers and squeezed hard.

"I don't think it would come to that between the two of you anyway," she said confidently. "But I know one thing for sure—you both need to not let anything or anyone from the outside cloud your judgment. You're making a mistake if you turn your back on Cade and your feelings for him because of past mistakes."

As if on cue, the front door opened and the sound of Cade's voice froze Nati.

"Okay, GiGi, I'm here. What is it that you need lifted that couldn't wait until tomorrow?"

Nati felt as if she were moving in slow motion when she turned her head just in time to see Cade come up short. He gawked at the scene in the living room for a moment.

Then his eyes honed in on his grandmother.

"What did you do?" he demanded.

Georgianna released Nati's hands and stood, raising a stubborn chin to the grandson who towered over her. "I hope I got you a second chance," she announced.

Then, clearly undaunted, she aimed her attention at Jonah and said, "How about a cup of coffee in the kitchen, Jonah?"

Nati's grandfather patted Nati's knee again then got

up to follow his old girlfriend, saying to Cade as he passed by him, "Your grandmother's made of steel—I always did like that about her. But there's a little of that in Nati, too. Getting through it is all up to you..."

And then there Nati was, still sitting on the sofa, alone in that big formal living room with Cade.

He was wearing old, faded, torn jeans and a sweatshirt—and yet he couldn't have looked better to her if he'd been in a tux.

He did look a little tired and stressed, though. Just like Nati.

"So... Do you want to fill me in?" he said, coming a few more steps into the living room.

Nati opted to stand, too, unsure what his response to her being there was. "I went to dinner with my grandfather. Afterward he said he had a surprise—and boy, did he! This is where I ended up."

"I'm sorry," Cade said, sounding genuinely apologetic. "Sometimes my grandmother..." He was obviously not happy with Georgianna. Aiming louder words in the direction of the kitchen he said, "When we were kids she always said we had to fight our own battles, apparently now she has no problem sticking her nose in where it doesn't belong."

"It's okay. She had a lot to say," Nati said.

"What exactly?"

Nati told him, rehashing it in her mind as she did, considering what the elder Camden had said, and if it had merit.

She realized along the way that it might. The message Cade had given her on Sunday night, the message her grandfather and Holly had repeated all week, and what Georgianna Camden had said just now all had a similar theme: judge Cade for the man he was. Nothing else should weigh on her decision.

Nati had had all week to think about her feelings for him. About why she was so devastated over losing him…

"I do think you're different from Doug. And maybe because your grandmother has the same roots my family has, you were raised with different values," Nati ventured.

"Have a little faith, Nati, that's all I'm asking," he said, repeating what he'd said on Sunday night.

But faith wasn't all she had to hang on to, she realized as she stood there.

During this last week she hadn't been able to stop thinking about Cade. She'd recalled certain moments that had given her clues to who he really was.

She'd recalled when he'd first met her grandfather and how respectful he'd been. It was nothing like the disdain and condescension that Doug and the Pirfoys had displayed when they'd been anywhere near her family.

She'd recalled the way Cade had behaved with Holly, with the other shop owners, even with the waitstaff in restaurants—again he'd shown only respect, friendliness, patience—never the kind of dismissal or superiority that she'd seen from the Pirfoys.

Cade's charm wasn't selective, the way Doug's had been. Cade was just Cade—he was the same person with her, with her grandfather, with Holly, with everyone.

Cade was a person who didn't turn up his nose at

eating pizza out of the box and drinking out of paper cups in her workroom. He was a person who pitched in when she'd needed help getting ready for the Scarecrow Festival. Doug would never have done that.

But the one very big difference between Cade and her ex was the responsibility that Cade showed. He actually worked in his family's business rather than merely cashing in on it. He honored his responsibilities to his family—here he was on a Friday night, answering a bogus summons from his grandmother for help. Nati hadn't seen any indications that he shirked his responsibilities. Rather than using the wealth at his disposal to escape from them the way Doug had, Cade met them head-on.

All these qualities were admirable and impressive. They'd won her over when they'd first met.

But that still didn't change how daunting it would be if things between them didn't work out, if she had to come up against all the firepower Camden money could buy…

"This still scares me…" she admitted with a glance at their surroundings.

"I know," he said soothingly. "And if GiGi had just cooled her jets a while longer and let me take care of things, I was coming to you with a plan. I've hired the four best divorce attorneys in the state to work together to write an ironclad prenuptial agreement for you. The platinum-standard of prenuptial agreements."

"For me, not for you?"

"Believe me, they think I'm crazy. But yeah, for you. You'll be able to beat me right over the head with it if you want to—"

"That *is* crazy—if I'm a gold digger—"

"I know you aren't. I told you, I have faith in you. And I love you—you didn't give me the chance to say that Sunday night, but it's true. I love you and I want you and I can't let what's standing in my way stop me. So I'll give you the big gun, then you don't have to worry about going up against me."

"You're really not afraid I'd just take the money and run?"

"I'm really not," he said calmly. "Because I think that we couldn't have ended up where we did if you didn't feel the same way about me that I feel about you. I think you have those feelings even against your better judgment. Even over and above your fears and worries and concerns."

He took a step nearer, smiling that slightly devilish smile that always got to her. "I saw all the hesitation in you. I had to engineer my way around it all. You didn't want to like me, but you did. You just couldn't help yourself because I'm so damn—"

"Arrogant and conceited?" she supplied to give him a hard time.

"I was going to say adorable."

Nati had to laugh at the sarcasm in that.

He took another step closer, nodding over his shoulder in the direction their grandparents had gone. "It looks like there aren't any hard feelings for us to worry about on that other count. You said yourself that I'm different from your ex. And as of next week I'll have a prenup for you that will ensure that you never have to worry. Am I still coming up against a no?"

He was standing close enough now that they were

nearly touching. Close enough for her to have to lift her chin high to look at him. Close enough to feel the heat of him. Close enough for every inch of her body to be crying out for his.

"You were only supposed to be the practice-guy," Nati said. "Some refresher-dating experience."

"Now, if you want it, you can have more than that..." he said, his voice a little raw, sounding for the first time the way he looked—ragged around the edges.

"I just want you..." she whispered as hot tears dampened her eyes for no reason except that he looked so good and she really did want him so much it hurt.

She saw some moisture collect in his eyes, too, just before he wrapped her in his arms and pulled her tightly to him.

"I love you so damn much..." he said, his emotion-laden words coming straight from the heart she could hear beating in his chest.

"I love you, too," she whispered against him.

He dropped a kiss to the top of her head but that wasn't enough for Nati. She raised her face to him and he wasted no time bringing his mouth to hers with an intensity that sealed them together and locked out everything else for a long while.

Together they were combustible. Not even the tenderness of the moment could keep things contained indefinitely. But this was certainly not the time or place for them to be getting stirred up...

Cade ended the kiss as if he were coming up for air. "So? *Will* you marry me?" he asked then.

"I will," Nati answered.

"And you'll spend the rest of your life with me? Because after this prenup I can't afford for you not to..."

She laughed. "Okay," she conceded.

"And there can be kids and grandkids and great-grandkids?"

"I hope so," she answered more softly, unable to think of the baby she'd lost.

"I'll make sure of it," Cade said, squeezing her a little before he kissed her again with so much passion she somehow knew they were going to have plenty of luck making babies.

He cut their kiss off a second time, though he seemed barely able to, and said, "We're gonna have to answer to those two conspirators in the kitchen. Then do you think your grandfather can get home on his own? Because I'm feeling the need to keep you captive from now until at least Sunday dinner."

"I'm pretty sure he can make it back by himself. Plus I don't know what's going on with them, but apparently there was a very long phone call that made them both feel like teenagers again—tonight might go on for a while for them, too."

"I'm not sticking around to chaperone," Cade declared.

"I don't think it'll go *that* far," Nati said confidently. Then she remembered the gleam in her grandfather's eyes when he'd looked at GiGi...

But she didn't tell Cade about that. Instead she said, "I'm sure we can just say good-night and go."

"In a minute, though," Cade said, holding her tight again. "I need just another minute."

Nati held him tight, too, her cheek securely to his chest.

It was as if Cade needed the imprint of her body against his to believe this was real, that it was going to last, that it wouldn't all go up in smoke any minute.

But as Nati stood there in his arms, her palms splayed across that broad, powerful back, she knew she didn't need any convincing that this was real.

Or right.

Or exactly where she was truly destined to be.

And suddenly the thought of the elaborate prenuptial agreement he was having written for her made her smile.

Because at that moment she knew to the very depths of her soul that this *would* last.

That in this man's arms was where she would begin and end the rest of her days.

And that there was nowhere else she would rather be.

No one else she would rather be with.

* * * * *